PRAISE FOR VAGABOND SOUTH PACIFIC

"Andersen's VAGABOND South Pacific offers historical short stories that are more fact than fiction and rightfully should be dubbed "faction". More than mere traveler's sagas he brings us stories that shock, astound and fascinate the reader all at the same time."

"Great stories with depth of meaning that evoke memories of Robert Louis Stevenson."

"Who knew the Solomon Islands are such a center of cultural richness, political shenanigans, outlandish behavior, pillage and indigenous rebellion. Andersen captures it all."

"VAGABOND South Pacific is full of real life characters making history in a part of the world too long ignored."

"Andersen's one-of-a-kind stories are set in remote places most of us can only dream about visiting, Tonga, Vanuatu, Samoa, The Solomon Islands, Fiji, Kiribati and New Caledonia. Somehow, he captures the essence of these small but culturally rich island nations in each of his fascinating tales. I finished the book in a long weekend wanting more."

ALSO BY GERALD R. ANDERSEN

Happily Married to a Chinese National

VAGA
SOUTH PACIFIC
BOND

Gerald R. Andersen

VAGABOND South Pacific Copyright © 2018 by Gerald R. Andersen. All Rights Reserved.

All rights reserved. No part of this book may be reproduced in any form or by any electronic or mechanical means including information storage and retrieval systems, without permission in writing from the author. The only exception is by a reviewer, who may quote short excerpts in a review.

Cover and interior design by Tess Andersen

This book is a work of fiction. Names, characters, places, and incidents either are products of the author's imagination or are used fictitiously. Any resemblance to actual persons, living or dead, events, or locales is entirely coincidental.

Gerald R. Andersen

Visit my website at **www.facebook.com/GeraldRAndersenAuthor**

Printed in the United States of America

First Printing: September 2018

ISBN-9781719882002

CONTENTS

1. Captain Cook's Tortoise — 2
2. Marry Her or Else, King Tupou's Birthday and Tongan Fireworks — 5
3. Home Is the Sailor Home From the Sea, Let's Fight — 23
4. Want Company? The Big Boom and Back In Time — 31
5. The Swede and Sweet Melani — 41
6. Sweet Melani and The Holy Mana Cult — 49
7. White Scarf Pilot and Submerged Cave Dwellers — 61
8. Flip Flop President and the Russians Are Coming — 71
9. Hanky Panky in The Oceanside Hotel — 79
10. Losing Sight and Where's The Man? Seppuku — 85
11. Jungle Bungee and Mr. And Mrs. Queen — 99
12. Moochers, Thieves and Island Detectives — 113
13. The Guesthouse: Caught Red-Handed, No Room at the Inn — 119
14. The Band Saw Massacre and Rite Of Passage — 129
15. Virgin Oil, Black Magic, You Cheat Me! — 139
16. Fire Bombs, Tear Gas and Assassination — 153

*Like all great travellers,
I have seen more than I remember,
And remember more than I have seen.*

—Benjamin Disraeli

*Remembering Terril Eikenberry
whose friendship exceeded all bounds
and whose honesty knew no limits.
He was a good man inside and out.*

INTRODUCTION

VAGABOND STORIES ARE SET IN ISLAND countries in the wet tropics. Tropical rain is a singular deluge. In the beginning it hints only faintly of what is to come. Often before we can find shelter, it is upon us. I have experienced tropical rain that didn't stop for 36 hours. It rained 36 inches in those 36 hours flooding fields, damaging roads and washing out bridges. But that is the extreme. It is usually a less damaging force. We all know it comes down in dogs, cats and buckets. But that isn't yet quite an apt description. Tropical rains flood streets, create instant streams in trails and swell streams turning them muddy brown within seconds. Downpour doesn't quite capture it either. To me tropical rain is like a cacophony of thousands of tiny hammers beating everything. Rain pelting down on corrugated, galvanized roofs sounds like a Jamaican steel drum band. Leaves rise and fall, splitter and spat. The rain lasts a few minutes or half an hour. Then as suddenly as it began, it is over. Like a car wash one moment all is awash. The next moment strong, warm winds provide a magnificent blow dry.

Travelers tend to think of the Pacific Islands as places with tropical breezes, trade winds and idyllic beaches where they sit under a beach umbrella in the sun and drink too much rum punch. The reality throughout the islands is ongoing conflict between the traditional family centered culture of sharing against the individualism, consumerism and avarice imposed by larger dominant countries and cultures. The principal change agents are immigrants encouraged by the long-term colonial rulers, Britain and France. These two countries together with Australia, New Zealand, China and the United States whose influence has been primarily through resource stripping, fishing and trade are transforming the Pacific Islands. When Americans and the Japanese invaded many Pacific Island countries in World War II bringing with them modern war material, equipment and products the traditional trade in commodities and raw material was instantly eclipsed. The native people, especially those in the Solomon Islands and Vanuatu, then known as the new Hebrides, developed an immediate fixation on the cargo that arrived, ostensibly for them, but had been expropriated by the invaders. While these stories are set decades after the emergence of cargo cults and the many attempts by locals to try to make cargo appear by creating miniature airports with airplane "decoys" and make beer appear by constructing wooden "refrigerators," the cargo cult mystique and the belief that somehow foreigners took cargo that belonged to Islanders remains.

Far from pacific, the Pacific Islands are hardly the tranquil paradise sold in tourism brochures. They are, in stark contrast, scenes of class and racial rivalry, and a clash of ancient, mainly paternal hierarchies, tribal traditions and structure with ever increasing "foreign" cultural influence. There continue to be strong political rivalries, coups, rebellions, independence movements and pressure to reduce traditional leaders' power. Some imposed changes, such as air travel, happen quickly. Some changes such as family dynamics, happen slowly. Indigenous traditions are not all good. Foreign traditions are not all bad. Islanders are still struggling to find their way.

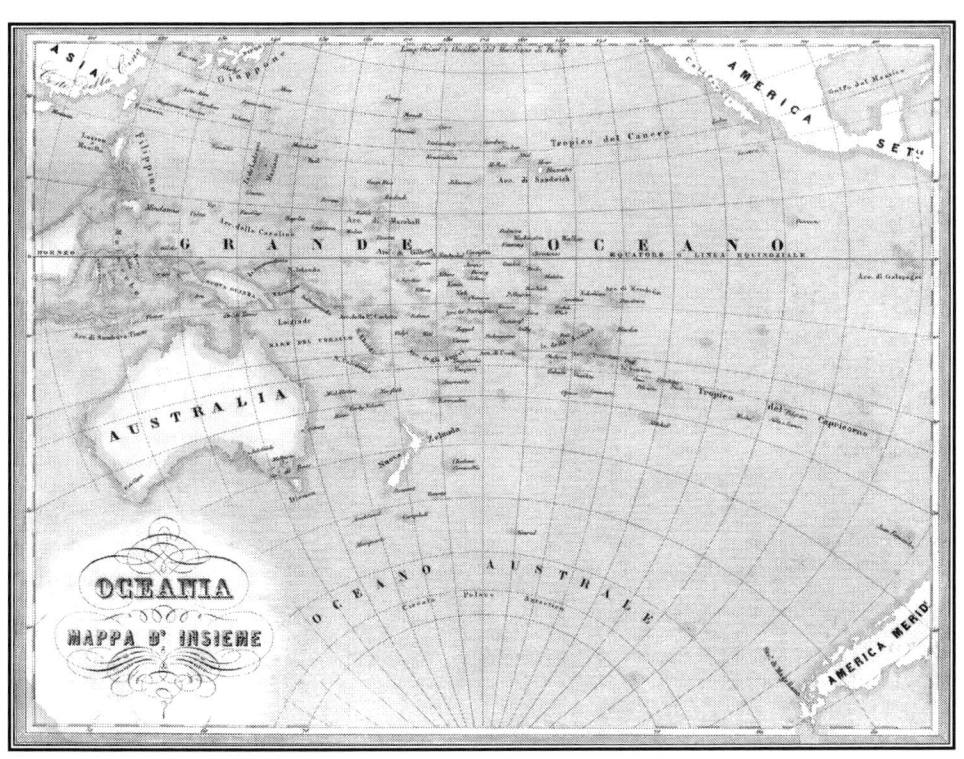

THE SOUTH PACIFIC
Oceania Mappa D'Insieme.
Genova. (1855).

VAGABOND

SOUTH PACIFIC

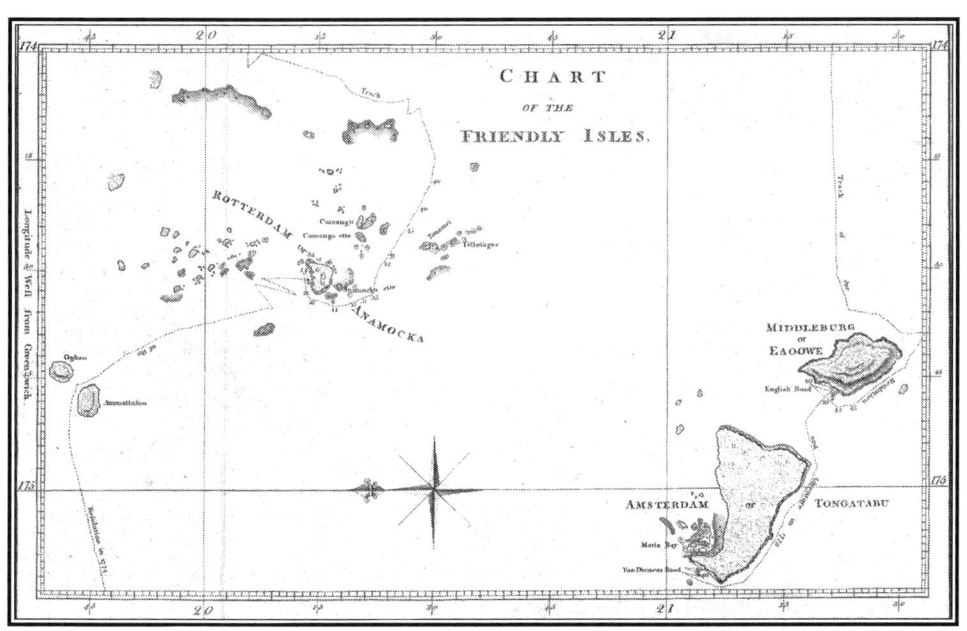

PART I: TONGA
Chart of the Friendly Isles.
No. XIV. Published Febry. 1st, 1777 by Wm. Strahan in New Street, Shoe Lane & Thos. Cadell in the Strand, London.

A night dance by women, in Hapaee.
J. Webber del. Wm. Sharp sculpt. (London, G. Nicol and T. Cadell, 1785)

Poulaho, King of the Friendly Islands.
J. Webber del. J. Hall sculp. (London, G. Nicol and T. Cadell, 1785)

Poulaho, King of the Friendly Islands, drinking kava.
J. Webber del. W. Sharp sculp. (London, G. Nicol and T. Cadell, 1785)

CHAPTER ONE

CAPTAIN COOK'S TORTOISE

TONGA

I calculated that if Captain Cook brought the tortoise to Tonga in 1777 the royal tortoise was 188 years old when it was killed. Wow, that tortoise was one of the longest-lived animals on earth. As I figured out the tortoise's age an enormous man garbed all in black with a pandanus woven mat wrapped around his torso came out of a side door and sat behind the reception desk.

AS SOON AS I WAS OLD ENOUGH to know better I felt mismatched with my name. Beginning in primary school my classmates would tease me about my name. I remember the sing-song taunting as if it were this morning. "Nyah, nyah, nyah, nyah, nyah. You've got a weird name. You've got a girl's name. You've got a stupid name. Nyah, nyah, nyah, nyah, nyah." Not wanting to insult my parents I waited until I reached my full 6 feet and my 18th birthday to request a legal name change.

Since my family came from Scandinavia I chose a particularly Nordic name, Nils. No longer would anyone tease me for having a feminine sounding name. From now on I would be known as Nils Torgersen. I would stand out because I am tall, lanky with blue eyes and dirty blond hair. No longer would I be noticed because of my name. No longer would anyone would call me Marion. I hated that name.

No one in university knew my old name nor did any of my adult friends. I didn't want to meet any of my childhood friends only to be taunted again. Other than to visit my parents, I had no contact with anyone in my hometown. None of my new friends knew about my past. I also promised myself to regret only some of the things I had done and not to regret things I had left undone. After the war, marriages, births, baptisms, graduations, divorces, retirements and deaths of my parents, those threads that stand out in the fabric of life, I vowed to see the world I had not yet seen.

That is where I came from so you'll understand my journey began decades ago.

At five o'clock somewhere on a windy day in July, I sat alone in a beach bar in Phuket, Thailand, contemplating the sun, the surf, the sand and my navel. As I watched the descending sun I decided to make a party for one. And to keep in theme ordered for my first drink a Fuzzy Navel. Waiting for the bartender, waiting for something brought to mind another July and another journey many years earlier.

☙❧

In a cool day in July in the middle of the South Pacific "winter" all those years ago, I boarded a flight in Nadi, Fiji bound for Nuku'alofa, Tonga. After a turbulent flight aboard one of Air Pacific's ATR 42s, I thought the flight should be renamed 'The Bump and Dump'. During the worst moments of the flight I recall watching the passengers' heads bob about like Indians agreeing with friends, or like one of those toys with the bobbing heads people affix to the rear window sills of their cars.

Upon landing in Tonga, I was so happy the flight was over, I was tempted, for a brief moment, to melodramatically kiss the ground at the bottom of the open-air exit stairs. But out of Scandinavian reserve, I resisted the urge.

After jostling with the huge Tongans and extracting my bag from the self-service baggage cart, I hailed a ramshackle taxi and once inside noticed the use of cut open beer boxes as floor mats. Before I could tell the driver where I was going he turned around, flashed a toothy smile, and said.

"Dateline Hotel?"

I confirmed the driver's hunch and in about 15 minutes was walking through the propped open door of the seen better days, clapboard Dateline Hotel on the waterfront in Nukualofa, Tonga. The island, called Tongatapu or sacred Tonga, is the home of the Kingdom's Royal family who live several hundred meters along the beach in a better maintained, clapboard, three story Victorian house which the proud Tongans call "The Palace."

As I waited for someone to show up to check me in I meandered around the lobby inspecting the rattan furniture and perusing tourism brochures until a glassed-in cabinet tucked behind the propped open entry doors caught my eye. As I walked closer I saw what appeared to be a stuffed turtle. Once at the door, I partially closed it and stepped closer to the display case to get a better view. What I thought was a turtle turned out to be a large stuffed tortoise poised with rocks and driftwood about three quarters of a meter long. I could barely make out the wording on a faded, painted sign in front of the tortoise.

"The Royal Tortoise, T'ui Malila, was killed by a car in 1965 when crossing the road. The tortoise was from Madagascar and a gift to the Tongan King from Captain James Cook during his Pacific voyage in July 1777."

I calculated that if Captain Cook brought the tortoise to Tonga in 1777 the royal tortoise was 188 years old when it was killed. Wow, that tortoise was one of the longest-lived animals on earth. As I figured out the tortoise's age an enormous man garbed all in black with a pandanus woven mat wrapped around his torso came out of a side door and sat behind the reception desk.

"Malo e lelei," the large man said. "Welcome. How can I help you?"

"Oh, hello, I'm checking in. Here is my reservation." I replied while walking to the reception desk and pulling from my backpack the emailed reservation I had printed on my home computer. I handed it to the imposing Tongan.

"Thank you. Yes, I see. We expect you Mr. Torgerson. Welcome to Nuku'alofa."

After checking in and unpacking, I decided to walk around Nuku'alofa. On this very quiet Sunday morning. I walked past a huge acacia tree and saw hundreds of bats hanging upside down. Their wings covered their bodies and shaded their eyes from the light. Inexplicably, I shuddered at the thought of so many bats. Little did I know the role those very bats would have the next day. Walking further I came upon a sandy graveyard with mounded graves. Several of the graves were framed with a symbolic fence of large beer bottles. Their necks stuck into the ground.

Though it was my first time in Tonga, I felt privileged to be there at the invitation of the Royal Family. Well sort of. A Baron, a member of the elite I had met, finagled an invite to the King's birthday celebration at the Palace the next day, July 4th. I was supposed to meet him there. I mean how often does one get invited to attend a King's birthday party?

CHAPTER TWO

MARRY HER OR ELSE, KING TUPOU'S BIRTHDAY AND TONGAN FIREWORKS

TONGA

"Ladies, and, of course, gentlemen....What you see before you skinned, prepared and roasted are reserved only for the King and his guests. It is an offense to eat one if not invited to the King's birthday and equally an offense not to eat one if you are."

Back at the hotel, I ate a simple chicken dinner with thick slices of taro and taro leaves cooked in coconut cream. Not tasty but filling and probably nutritious.

After reading a Pacific Islands news magazine I purchased at the airport in Fiji, I crawled into bed and watched and listened to the slowly rotating ceiling fan. Covered with only a sheet I wished for air conditioning. Soon the hot humid air made me sleepy though I remember tossing and turning in the night and slapping at a mosquito.

Somewhere in the distance of my dream a rooster crowed, then again as I drifted in and out of my morning slumber. Quickly the grayness of dawn became streaks of light through the partially closed curtains. Before I fully realized, it was morning the tropical sun shone bright and flooded the room with light.

At a late breakfast the dining room was full of officials and diplomats I recognized from the flight from Nadi. They likely also had been invited to attend the King's birthday party beginning at six o'clock that evening at the Palace. At breakfast I tried some Australian Vegemite on my toast for the first time. After one bite I said out loud "ghastly" and wondered how people could eat it. It tasted like I imagined axle grease would taste. I decided it was a taste acquired only as a child.

After a third cup of coffee I was, except for a waiter, alone in the dining room. Evidently, everyone else had business or appointments. Given that my entire day was free I decided to explore more of the town.

After wandering about the nondescript downtown for a couple of hours, I returned to saunter along the beach. Following a leisurely 20 minutes-walk past the "Palace" I came to a small house grandly named the Beachside Café and Guesthouse. I decided to stop and have lunch and there met Mrs. Finau and her children, a primary school girl, Salote, and a high school age girl named Kalasia. Both had two long braids tied with white ribbons. After serving me lunch, and as I was the only customer, Mrs. Finau sat at my table and begin to converse. The girls ran back and forth through the screened porch dining room cradling newly born, squealing piglets as if they were kittens or puppies. It did not take long for me to learn the family history, that Mrs. Finau was a widow and in addition to the girls had an older son who worked at a local Ministry office. She had started the guesthouse and café after her husband's death to support the family. After she finished her story and was asking me about my family, an obviously very pregnant young woman came through the front door.

"Hello mother," she said. "I hope you are doing well. It is good to see you this morning."

After the young woman walked through the porch into the house, I heard the clatter of dishes being washed.

"I thought you said you had only three children?" I questioned. "Who is this other young woman who calls you mother?"

"Oh she is Lovai, my daughter-in-law. Her name means beloved in Tongan. But my son Lotu, meaning admired in Tongan, did not want to marry her even though he made her pregnant. I told him that if he did not marry her he would not be admired. I said 'you must love her and make her feel cherished and loved. If you do not I will go to the town and sell myself to strangers.'

He was so shocked. I shamed him enough to marry her. I am happy he still listens to his mother. Lovai is a good girl.

Look at my daughters, Kalasia and Salome, who is named after our only queen. They are only girls but both the past and future are in them. I have never been outside Tonga and even in Tonga I have only been to Va'vau. So, I don't know about other girls and women from outside. But I know that in the soul of every Tongan girl is a woman who wants to be cherished and loved every day. And inside every cherished and loved Tongan woman is a girl who wants to play.

Lotu does not yet know these things because he was too young to learn these things before his father died. But I know because my husband, Viliami, cherished and loved me like that. Lovai will teach Lotu. He can learn. He has a good heart. Some men never learn. They are unhappy and their wives are unhappy because the husband does not know how to love his wife. Leaving and getting another woman won't change anything. He still won't know how to cherish his wife. The new woman will be unhappy too because she is with him."

After I paid Mrs. Finau, I didn't know what to say other than make polite noises.

"Thank you for your kind hospitality and for the delicious meal. It was good getting to know you and your family. I am going to the King's birthday celebration and need to return to my hotel to get ready. Again, it was delightful to meet your family."

"Thank you. Oh, that is an honor to be invited to the King's birthday. I have never been. But you may see my daughters there."

"Really? Are they guests too?"

"Well not exactly. But I hope you will see them. Enjoy the party!"

After a nap, I was to be at the Palace at 6 o'clock. I expected a reception in the grounds. But as I was soon to learn, it was altogether different.

After lunch at the Beachside Café I continued to walk along the waterfront. As the beach was closed off in front of the palace, I walked around the picket-fenced palace grounds and came upon soldiers jogging behind a black Mercedes 500.

Before I knew what was happening several of the soldiers stood in front of me and blocked my way. As a very large man got out of the long limousine, one of the guards retrieved a small folding bicycle from the trunk of the Mercedes. As the man begin to ride on the bicycle, I noticed he was so huge that the bicycle seat disappeared when he sat on it. As he pedaled and the bicycle began to move forward, the soldiers jogged alongside either side of him. I didn't quite know what to make of it but later learned I had stumbled upon the King exercising.

Later that evening invitation in hand, I walked from the Dateline Hotel along with a group of others toward the Palace. There I joined the queue at the palace gate of suited expatriates and local grandees dressed in formal tapa "skirts" wrapped with voluminous pandanus mats. I was expecting a typical cocktail reception in the palace grounds but was taken aback at what happened next.

After my invitation was inspected a Tongan man in a military uniform approached me and looked at my invitation again.

"Mr. Nils Torgerson would you please be so kind as to follow me to the beach. Once we are at the beach there are chairs with red ribbons and green ribbons. You may sit in any of the green ribbon chairs. The red ribbon chairs closest to the King are for the Barons and their families."

Once I was on the beach, the military man returned to the gate. I found myself surrounded by expatriates and could not help overhearing the group talking next to me.

"Well, this is my second time to attend the King's birthday celebration," a man with a British accent began. "Let me tell you. Like it or hate it, it is something you'll never forget. But you must remember to be polite."

"Whatever do you mean?" A woman standing next to him questioned. "Of course, we'll be polite. We're British."

"I shan't let the cat out of the bag," he continued. But as for British politeness, my dear, that remains to be seen."

Wending my way through the crowd of military men, pandanus clad Tongans and overseas expatriates, I approached a coconut palm, woven, thatch covered structure paralleling the beach. I estimated it to be four hundred feet long. The frame, made of bamboo poles was held together with coconut fiber twine tied in geometric black and brown patterns. Once inside the structure I was most impressed by what I saw next.

A hundred seats tied with red or green ribbon were positioned with backs against the coconut palm thatched walls. Each seat was covered with white tapa cloth I knew was hand made by pounding mulberry bark. Each cover was painted in black and brown geometric designs. All the seats faced the ocean and a single, long table. But the seats we're not chairs at all in the western sense but small raised back supports placed on top of long, soft pandanus mats.

The table, covered in coconut palm mats, stretched for at least 300 hundred feet. Between place settings was a small bouquet of multi-colored flowers. In front of the center of the table where the King would sit on a large tapa covered chair was an elaborate six-foot-long arrangement of orchids, plumeria and ferns.

As I looked along the table for a seat and just as I spotted a free seat with a green ribbon attached I saw Mrs. Finau's two daughters, Salote and Kalasia, whom I met earlier in the day. They saw me too but only returned my gaze and smiled. The two playful girls I had come to know during lunch were dressed in white tapa dresses and intently listening to an older woman who was evidently instructing them.

As all the guests found places at the table, I noticed that the Brit I overheard earlier sat only two seats away.

Just as I noticed that no one was sitting in any of the seats tied with red ribbons, Tongans, clad in tapa and wrapped in pandanus aprons, began to arrive, remove their shoes and take their places. I noticed that expatriates, who had not done so, quickly removed their shoes as did I. At the same time a troop of young girls walked in. Each one bowed her head in respect as she passed in front of a guest. Once in position, the girls remained standing until all the girls were in their respective places. Then they bowed in unison, removed their shoes and sat on the pandanus mats placed in front of the tables facing the guests, their backs to the ocean.

One girl sat between each of two guests. Each girl carried a triangular fan with a three-foot-long handle. I was puzzled as to what their roles would be but quickly found out when the girls began to fan the guests ever so slowly like a Tongan version of an Indian punkah wallah.

Again, the Brit I had overheard earlier opined to his colleagues.

"The girls you just saw are one of the most delightful parts of the celebration. You'll note they are careful not to point their feet at the guests so as not to insult them. They will sit in position and fan us the entire evening. When the food is served, you'll learn about their second function. If you look to the left you'll see where the men cook in umus or earth ovens. Traditionally, Tongans will cook whole pigs, vegetables, chickens, fish, green bananas, taro, yams, and sweet potatoes. Some of those things will come from those umus today. The men started this whole process many hours ago. I've heard the temperature in the umus gets to be 1000 degrees Fahrenheit or more."

Looking to the left along the beach, I saw a dozen large men gathered around several smoking mounds in the earth, evidently the umus.

The Brit continued, "on the right, you'll see women preparing seaweed salads, raw fish and octopus marinated in lemon juice and coconut cream. None of those dishes will be served until after the main course reserved only for the King."

"Wow food fit for a King," a red headed woman next to him exclaimed.

"Well food for a Tongan King at least," the Brit responded. "We shall see."

"Well as long as the King serves cocktails, I'll be alright."

"That won't happen. Not at this function. Most of the Tongans including the nobles here tonight are strict teetotalers. There won't be cocktails, nor beer nor wine today. Enjoy the endless supply of fresh coconut water which they'll begin delivering, though don't drink too much. I've been told it is both a diuretic and a laxative."

After hearing this, I made a mental note not to drink too much as I had not seen any kind of a toilet nearby.

"Oh look," the Brit exclaimed, "they are opening some of the umus. Soon they will be serving the first course. Once the food is served the girls will be sure to keep the flies off the food as well as attempt to fan the guests. I can hardly wait to see how much you'll enjoy the food fit for a King." He spoke to no one in particular and everyone.

"I can hardly wait," said the redhead.

"Nor can I," retorted the Brit.

A group of about 50 Tongans all dressed in black, the women in ground length tapa dresses, lined up in neat rows directly in front of us, their backs to the ocean. As they began to sing the Tongans stood up. The expatriates followed suit in anticipation that the King was about to arrive. The Tongans sang a' Capella in four-part harmony.

> *Oh, Almighty God above,*
> *Though art our Lord and sure defense*
> *In our goodness we do trust Thee*
> *And our Tonga Thou dost love;*
> *Hear our prayer, for though unseen*
> *We know that Thou hast blessed our land;*
> *Grant our earnest supplication,*
> *and save Tupou our King.*

I noticed that many of the women began to cry during the song. At the end of the song the choir went silent as King Tupou entered the enclosure. At 6 feet 5 inches tall, dressed in pure white tapa, wrapped in pandanus and weighing more than four hundred pounds, he could only be described as imposing. He approached his place in the middle of the table and lowered himself ponderously into his very strongly built beach throne. After he was seated, the choir began singing both hymns and Tongan folk songs.

Soon the men near the umus carried stretcher sized trays of food to the serving tables at each end of the long table. While difficult to see clearly in the dimming light, the trays appeared to be laden with dozens of small roasted piglets. The women brought the first plate to the King, the royal family seated next to the King and to nobles sitting at the seats with red ribbons. Thereafter, they served those at the seats with green ribbons.

Though the men had lit torches around the enclosure, it was difficult at first to see what the woman served me as she nodded her head respectfully and placed a plate in front of me and the guests on either side.

It didn't take long for me to find out; however, as the Brit began an explanation of what they were about to eat.

"Ladies, and, of course, gentlemen," he whispered, "before I tell you about the food before us that we must eat, I must remind you that everyone, including the girls opposite, are watching for any sign of displeasure and listening for any word which may show disrespect for the King. It will also do no good to say that you are a vegetarian though what you're about to eat certainly is. What you see before you skinned, prepared and roasted are reserved only for the King and his guests. It is an offense to eat one if not invited to the King's birthday and equally an offense not to eat one if you are. These small mammals are not baby piglets but fully mature fruit bats. The same fruit bats that hang from the trees by day. They all belong to the King and are served to non-royals only on his birthday. Enjoy."

"I don't think I can," said the redhead.

"Penelope, you can and you will. Members of the British High Commission must sacrifice not only their livers but also their stomachs for Queen and country. Think of England and carry on."

After, the women ceremoniously placed multiple courses before us including not only fruit bat, but raw marinated fish, octopus in coconut milk, seaweed salad and fern salad, I thought I had sacrificed quite enough. The nobles left immediately after the King who stayed only about two hours. The girls maintained their positions as long as their guests remained. After I left my place at the table I looked in vain for the two girls, Salote and Kalasia.

"I," said to myself out loud, "must take a walk."

Strolling down to the water's edge I sat on a smooth rock and looked across at the islands in the distance. As I sat there Salote and Kalasia appeared and sat beside me.

"Wasn't it exciting?" Salote began. "But the best part is yet to come. Fireworks."

"Fireworks?" I questioned. "I don't see any fireworks."

"Oh yes," Salote replied. "You must look more closely across the water toward the islands. There are only a few now. Soon there will hundreds of fireworks to honor the King. This is the first year we get to serve at King Tupou's Birthday but I have been watching the fireworks since I was little."

I looked upwards and still saw nothing. "Nope nothing"

The nine-year-old beauty, Salote, chastised me. "Oh, you silly. You'll never see fireworks in the sky. Look on the beaches. That is where they light the fires. Look!"

She said with a broad smile. "There are more and more fireworks. It is so beautiful. If you want to see beautiful things you need to know where to look."

I gazed back at her the longest time appreciating her beauty and her innocent wisdom.

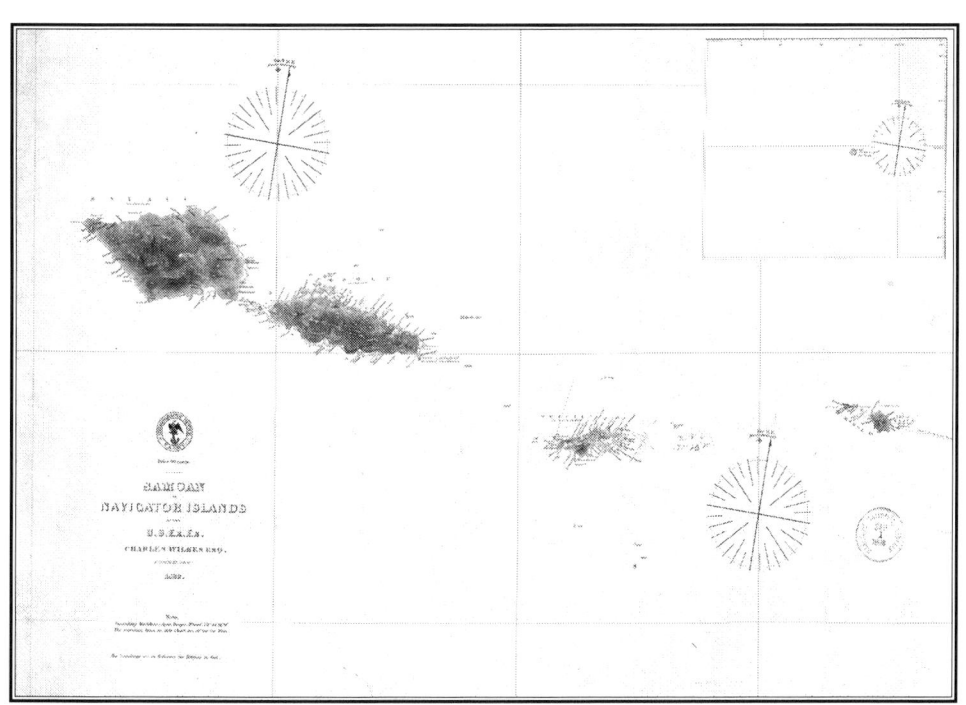

PART II: SAMOA
Samoan or Navigator Islands.
Washington: Hydrographic Office. Hydrographic Office (Navy). (1900).

Ficus or Banyan tree. Upolu.
Drawn by A.T. Agate. Engd. by Rawdon, Wright & Hatch. (Philadelphia: Lea & Blanchard. 1845)

Massacre of De Langle, Lemanon & Ten Others of the Two Crews.
Published as the Act directs Novr. 1st 1798,
by G.G. & J. Robinson, Paternoster Row. Heath Sculp. No. 66.

CHAPTER THREE

HOME IS THE SAILOR HOME FROM THE SEA, LET'S FIGHT

SAMOA

Suddenly, the room went silent. It was as if time stood still as everyone stood frozen in place. Then from across the room came the sound of a raucous, belly laugh from the man William had greeted. After that everyone in the room exploded into laughter.

BACK IN FIJI AT THE BEACH BAR at Club Fiji I finished the string of Ratu's Plantation Rum drinks and headed for the airport to take another flight in the Pacific Islands. But this time I am traveling to Samoa to see where Robert Louis Stevenson lived and wrote.

The Pacific Islands have fascinated me ever since I began reading Robert Louis Stevenson novels as a boy. Since I retired I am determined to retrace his steps or at least visit some of the places Stevenson wrote about, traveled to or lived. And that is I why I will stay at the Tusitala Hotel in Apia, Samoa where Stevenson lived and was buried. Tusitala, meaning story teller in Samoan, is the name the Samoans gave Stevenson. The hotel is named after him.

I reflected about how this journey to Samoa began. Before coming to Samoa, I went to a small port city, Everett, north of Seattle on Puget Sound on the United States west coast. That, of all places, is where one goes to see Stevenson's boat, The Equator. When I was researching Stevenson, I learnt that the Equator was built in 1888 in Benicia, California. Though originally a schooner when Stevenson chartered the boat, it was later converted to a tug boat. The wood plank Equator ended up in Puget Sound and was beached on a jetty to act as part of a breakwater near the mouth of the Snohomish River. Except for an observant high school student who found her in the mid 1960s, she may have ended her days there. As it happened, local citizens and a salvage operator got her off the breakwater and refloated her. Though unrestored, the Equator now rests under the roof of an open-air building at the 14th Street dock in Everett, Washington USA.

The evening I arrived in Samoa, I met the new U.S. Peace Corps Director to Samoa, William Farman in the dining room of the hotel. He was staying in the Tusitala Hotel as well until his house was ready and his furnishings arrived. I thought him a nice enough guy and was especially thankful to be invited to accompany him to a welcome reception for him that evening at Robert Louis Stevenson's home, Vailima. Otherwise, I might never get to see inside.

After breakfast, and as it was a lazy Saturday, I decided to climb up to Stevenson's tomb on the top of a steep hill next door to Stevenson's house before the sun made the effort too hot and miserable. As I set out I made sure to take sun lotion and mosquito spray in addition to my broad brimmed travel hat which also covers the back of my neck. As I look at myself in the mirror before I set out, I look just like a typical tourist.

"I don't care. I am a tourist." I said out loud. After getting directions, I got a map from the hotel and set out carrying a small bottle of water.

Walking along the waterfront I noticed the gray government building with the painted over half-timbered construction, a remnant of German colonial days. As I passed, about a dozen tall and chubby Samoans holding brass instruments and drums assembled at the base of the flagpole in front of the two-story government building and began to play brass instruments including a tuba to make German oom pah music as one of them raised the flag. It was funny, I thought. Samoa ceased being a German protectorate at the outbreak of World War I yet the locals obviously still hung on to some German traditions including the band members' pith helmets.

About three miles from town and after crossing the fields and streams at the base of Mount Vaea where Stevenson's tomb is, I looked for a sign pointing the way to Stevenson's grave. I found none but after walking part way around the base of the hill I saw a narrow trail which appeared to lead upwards. I followed it and after about an hour neared the top where, after pushing aside some brush, I found a crude, concrete tomb. The words of the inscribed epitaph from Stevenson's poem "Requiem" were not clear but I knew it by heart.

Under the wide and starry sky,
Dig the grave and let me lie
Glad did I live and gladly die,
And I laid me down with a will
This be the verse you grave for me,
Here he lies where he longed to be;
Home is the sailor home from the sea,
And the hunter home from the hill

—***Robert Louis Stevenson***

At first, I think the grave too humble, too ignominious for such a great author but after I rest and view the sea I realize that this resting place even this crude grave would suit Stevenson just fine. Here he lies where he longed to be.

Though I intended to return the Tusitala Hotel by lunch I had underestimated the distance, the speed I could walk and how often I needed to rest in the tropical heat.

Feeling dehydrated after hiking down from Stevenson's grave I notice a small cafe and decide to get something to drink. Inside I order coconut water with ice to quench my thirst.

I sat at a small table near the door away from the rest of the patrons sipping my drink and minding my own business when a large Samoan swaggered toward my table.

"Palagi, I don lie you. Lezz go outsie an figh righ now."

"Oh, I'm not a fighter," I replied. "I'm just leaving anyway," and got up to leave.

"No, no, no, no," he shouted shaking his fist at me. "We gonna figh."

As the big Samoan lurched toward me, two other Samoans put their hands on his shoulders and restrained him.

"Tito, come and have another beer." The younger of them said while coaxing Tito away by holding a beer just out of his reach.

"Sorry 'bout Tito," explained the older man. "He wants to fight with everyone when he gets drunk. But good idea you go."

After leaving I thought about this close call as later I showered and dressed for the Peace Corps Director's welcome reception beginning at 5:00 PM at Robert Louis Stevenson's home, Vailima.

The young American Peace Corps Director, William, and I shared a taxi from the Tusitala Hotel to the reception. Before we entered, he told me what to expect.

"I've been told that most of the Cabinet Ministers and many members of parliament will be at the reception this evening. I met one of the Ministers today at lunch. His nickname is Ofa. He said he would introduce me. I'm really hyped."

I fell in behind the Peace Corps Director as we entered Stevenson's house through the ajar double doors. Seeing his new friend across the room, William waved at him and yelled out a hearty greeting.

"Hello Ufa."

Suddenly, the room went silent. It was as if time stood still as everyone stood frozen in place.

Then from across the room came the sound of a raucous, belly laugh from the man William had greeted. After that everyone in the room exploded into laughter.

William looked at me totally bewildered as Ofa walked toward us from across the room.

"William, you may wonder why everyone went silent when you greeted me. My name is Ofa with an O. You called me Ufa with a U. In Samoan that word means asshole. Now you know your first Samoan word. I think you definitely broke the ice. Welcome to Samoa."

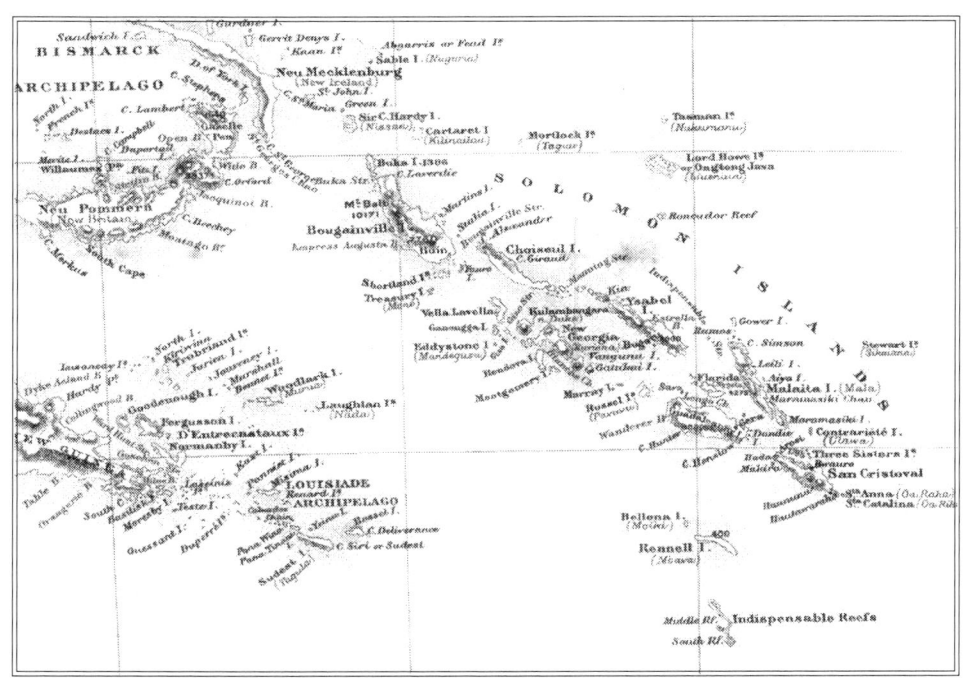

PART III: SOLOMON ISLANDS
Melanesia.
London. (1912).

CHAPTER FOUR

WANT COMPANY? THE BIG BOOM AND BACK IN TIME

SOLOMON ISLANDS

"I can see you are drinking incognito," the man seated next to me began. "I mean that monstrosity looks like a bloated Brazilian carnival dancer. Definitely not low key. It's meant for the girls. You should man up and drink some whisky straight or just order a beer if you know what I mean. Don't get your knickers in a twist, I'm just funning with you. My name's Kurt with a K. What's yours?

THE AIR SOLOMONS FLIGHT TO HONIARA was uneventful. I had done my homework before boarding in Fiji. Having read several articles about the early history of the Solomon Islands, I was delighted to check into the Mendana Hotel named after the Spanish Explorer, Captain Alvaro de Mendana y Naira whom I had just been reading about. Mendana sailed into Guadalcanal with his wife, Dona Isabel, in 1595 with the ill-fated intention of becoming King of a new Spanish colony. Mendana named the Islas Salomon, later shortened to the Solomon Islands, during an earlier voyage to the islands in 1568. The 1595 voyage to the Solomons was Mendana's last as he died there in October 1595.

His vain wife was left in charge and abandoned the colony within a month after Mendana's death. She hoarded food while others aboard her ship starved to death enroute to Manila. Except for a Spanish voyage in 1607, no outsider visited the Solomons for 150 years.

After check-in and a shower, I went for a walk along the waterfront in the fading light before dinner. Almost as soon as I left the hotel I saw a sign sponsored by the Lion's Club of Guadalcanal which implored the public to:

Keep Honiara Clean, Healthy and Beautiful. Head lice dogs and cats. All families must have cats in their houses. Make rats your enemies - Kill them. Kill all roaming dogs and keep your licensed dogs secure at home. Keep hair short and clean.

Chuckling to myself about the public service message I walked for about half an hour enjoying the fragrance of the Frangipani trees along the road. As I began to return to the hotel I heard a female voice.

"You, you. Psst. Psst. Look over here on the side of the road. I can see you. You Chinese? I like Chinese. You see me? You want company?"

I saw no one but I answered the unseen voice to discourage any further offers I didn't want to hear.

"No, I'm not Chinese," I replied impatiently to the unseen voice "and no I don't want any company." After that I heard no further voices and returned to the Mendana Hotel.

After a nondescript dinner, I walked a few paces toward the Oceanview bar. Craving more to eat and something sweet I ordered some cashews and a rum coconut drink called Pacific Sunset. I was surprised a few minutes later when the bartender placed in front of me a full-sized, unhusked coconut the size of a football decorated with a foot-long curly cue purple straw, a one-foot long skewer of tropical fruit, a florescent pink palm tree swizzle stick and a large yellow paper umbrella.

"I can see you are drinking incognito," the man seated next to me began. "I mean that monstrosity looks like a bloated Brazilian carnival dancer. Definitely not low key. It's meant for the girls. You should man up and drink some whisky straight or just order a beer if you know what I mean. Don't get your knickers in a twist, I'm just funning with you. My name's Kurt with a K. What's yours?

"Oh, I'm not offended. My name's Nils with an N. I think this drink looks ridiculous as well. It made me think of a Latin dancer in the old reruns my dad used to watch on TV. I think her name was Carmen Miranda. She used to wear hats that looked like this drink."

"I remember hearing her name but never saw her act. That was way before my time. What brings you to Honiara, some kind of government work?"

"No nothing like that. I'm retired and resolved not to regret not doing things only to regret some things I have done. So here I am."

"Heh, heh, heh. This place may be one of those things you come to regret. It's weird. Some people find it fascinating. I find a lot of things here hard to reconcile. But then I'm jaded. I'm a deminer by profession, former British Army Ordinance."

"Deminer huh? That's like the bomb squad guys, right?"

"Sort of. Here I mostly deal with unexploded World War II ordinance which we call UXO. I deal with mines too but for me that work is mostly in Laos. During the

Vietnam war you Yanks dropped more bombs and mines in Laos than anywhere else. It's arguably the most mined and bombed place on earth. Deminers will be working there for a hundred years."

"You're kidding. 100 years, that can't be right."

"Think about it! We're still working here 75 years after the end of World War II."

"Oh right! You have a really dangerous job. What does your wife think about it?"

"Far as I know she still doesn't like it but I haven't talked to her for about 20 years. We never had kids and split in the last century. Marriage and demining do not mix well. I'd be gone half the time and the rest of the time my wife just thought about what she used to call the 'Big Boom'. I told her with my luck it'd be on my last day of work so not to worry."

"I imagine whenever that 'Big Boom' day comes it will indeed be your last day of work."

"Yeah, well that is one of the many reasons I still rent a house in Northern Thailand. After two weeks working in Laos, I go to my house and do what the bar girls there call 'Boom, Boom' if you know what I mean. Ha...ha...ha....We deminers work hard but we party hard too."

"So, you only work here periodically?"

"Pretty much. Whenever locals or divers report ordinance the authorities call my office and I or one of my mates come down here 'to diffuse' the situation. I've been coming down here for about 15 years now so many of the locals know me pretty well. I've even been invited to some of their homes when I work in some of the more remote islands. Some weird things go on out there. In fact, I'm scheduled to go day after tomorrow. If you're interested you could tag along. I have to warn you though the boat rides can get pretty hairy."

"I'd love to do that," I replied. "Tell me more."

"Enough about me. We can talk more during the boat trip in a couple of days. You should go out to Swede's for dinner some evening. He's an institution around here. Been in the Solomons forever. He's older than God. He's on his third wife. Gossip is he keeps wearing them out. He's got a gaggle of kids most of whom have gone to university. Someday they'll probably run the country. I know him because he also used to be a deminer. He first came here in the 60s and being smarter than me, married his first wife, stopped tempting fate every day and started a business. It's no gold mine but it's a living. His youngest, Melani still works at the resort. In fact, I understand he's got several businesses now. I can't keep track.

"Sounds interesting," I replied. "Can you give me directions?"

"Directions? You won't need directions. Just turn right and drive up the coast road in front of the Mendana until it ends. His resort, if you can call four cabins a resort, is on the oceanside hidden behind a lot of trees. Can't miss it." He advised over his shoulder while walking out of the bar, "Sorry to leave so soon but I almost forgot I'm supposed to keep someone company if you know what a mean? Hmmm?"

The next afternoon a local, sporting what I can only describe as dreadlocks, with a snaggle tooth, wearing a Jim Hendrix t-shirt, orange shorts, beach sandals and twirling car keys around his index finger approached me in the dining room. He addressed me in the local Pijin. It's pretty necessary since the Solomon Islanders speak more than 70 languages.

"Nem blong yu, Mista Nils?"

"Yes, I'm Nils. How do you know it's me?"

"Nem blong mi, Peni. Big Man Car Hire. Yu spik Pijin?"

"I don't understand."

"No problem I spik English Mista Nils. Not many in town wan hire car. If dey lif here dey don need. If dey tourist, dey go with driver. My fren work long hotel. Hem think you are long timer but I don know. Sorry. You got Suzuki Jeep "

"Oh excellent, Peni. Any paperwork?"

"No worry. Sapos I kam baek yu two days Mr. Nils? Yu agri."

Somehow, I understood the mixture of Pijin and English and answered "I agree."

Coming out of the hotel parking lot I followed Kurt's directions, turned right and drove the seen-better-days Suzuki Jeep along the coast road toward Mangakaki. The two-lane road quickly becomes a dirt track after it runs out of Honiara past the World War II, American built, Hendersen Field, Solomon's only International airport. After the war the British Colonial administration required Allied Forces to plow excess war material into landfills and into Iron Bottom Bay so as not to disrupt the local economy. To this day, U.S. military personnel and contractors like Kurt still remove unexploded ordinance (UXO) and search for the remains of American troops killed during the battle of Guadalcanal which ended in February 1943.

The slow Mangakaki dirt track is lined with senile coconut palms planted by Lever Brothers decades ago. While Lever Brothers, later called Unilever, only had plantations on about 20,000 acres in the Solomons, at one time the company controlled up to 400,000 acres on 99 to 999-year leases. The road followed the coast, crossed several rivers spanned with decades old, temporary Bailey Bridges and became a single lane road about an hour out of town. For the entire drive I saw few houses and only half a dozen locals along the road. I noticed the sky clouding over as the road narrowed to a single track and degraded the further I drove. The road ended abruptly at sand dunes and a trail too narrow for a car.

Kurt was right. No directions were needed. There to my right behind some trees that reached almost to the ground I saw some rustic, small cabins clustered around a pond. To the right of them closer to the beach I saw what appeared to be the main building. Leaving the car in the middle of the road when I couldn't drive any further, I walked toward the entrance.

As I entered the building I felt like I had gone back in time. The bamboo walled, palm thatched structure had no glass windows only openings with shutters propped open with bamboo sticks. The sparse furniture was crafted from rattan and the tables had flattened bamboo tops exactly the same material as the walls. In one corner stood an elaborate, obviously imported, Peacock chair with a prominent Do Not Sit Here sign. I saw no staff nor customers and decided to choose a table at a window on the oceanside. As I did so a part European Melanesian girl entered and began to light kerosene hurricane lamps on each table and a larger one hanging from the center of the room.

"Good evening. Welcome to Swede's," she began in perfect English. "Dinner is roast pork with veg. Starter is fresh Wahoo fish marinated in lemon juice and coconut milk with chilis followed by fruit salad with sweet pandanus. Will you be having a drink? We have beer, vodka, gin and rum, fruit juice, and fresh coconut. Filtered water is in the jug on your table. There is no ice. We don't have a generator."

As I thought about the choices as she continued her preparations. It didn't take me long to realize there were no choices except what to drink.

Remembering what Kurt had said the night before about manning up I replied, "may I have a beer please?"

"Yes, it is Victoria Bitter from Australia," she replied preparing to leave the room.

Before she could leave I couldn't help but ask a question. "Are you Melani by chance? I don't mean to be impolite but I met Kurt at the Mendana. He's the one who told me to come here for dinner."

"It's OK. And yes, I am Melani. Kurt is a good friend of my father who is quite old now. I am his youngest child. I have helped him operate the resort since I finished school. None of my brothers or sisters want to work here so my mother and I do because it is my father's dream. And we want to help fulfill his dream. I'll go to get your drink.

After she left the dining room, I sat in silence listening to the waves lap the shore. After she brought my beer, I walked out onto the beach bending down to walk under the tree branches hugging the black sand beach. The only sounds were the surf and cicadas calling each other. I could see the flutter of wings from the occasional bat and as I thought about all the soldiers who died decades earlier on these now peaceful beaches a heat contraction flash roused me from such thoughts. Without thinking I began counting 1001,1002,1003 waiting for the sound of thunder. I counted to 1010 before I heard the crack of thunder then decided to go back inside in case of rain.

Melani appeared from the kitchen with a sea clam shell filled with the starter, fish marinated in lemon juice and coconut milk with tomatoes, onions and green chilies and placed it on the table in front of me.

"This looks delicious. Is it the same dish the Fijians call Kokoda?"

"Yes," Melani replied. "In fact, my mother learnt this recipe from a Fijian. Everyone likes it. Well everyone who likes raw fish likes it."

"Any chance your father will be here this evening?"

"It's always possible but don't count on it. If he does you will notice. He always sits in the Peacock chair. He calls it his Sydney Greenstreet soliloquy whatever that means."

CHAPTER FIVE

THE SWEDE AND SWEET MELANI

SOLOMON ISLANDS

They pay big bribes to officials in Honiara to get permits. Traditional landowners are not consulted or given almost nothing. It has been going on since I was child. The loggers take our young girls and even the young boys into the camps and onto the ships. Some of them falsely marry very young girls by paying parents a bride price. The loggers abandon the girls and their children when they leave the Solomons.

AS I WAS ABOUT TO TUCK INTO THE ROAST pork and vegetables, a stately European man, slightly hunched over and dressed all in white except for the black band on his Panama hat strolled into the almost empty dining room and strode toward the peacock chair. I thought...this is Swede, the guy Kurt had told me about and the owner of the resort. I'll get a chance to meet him I thought.

Turning toward him, I said, "Sir, pardon me. I'm here because your friend Kurt told me about your resort. I met Melani. My name is Nils Torgerson."

"Kurt huh? Ahhhh. I can tell you're an American and a Scandinavian too eh? Good to meet you. I'm Swenson but call me Swede everyone else does. Hope you are enjoying my wife's cooking. It's wholesome, local and organic long before such things became the pathetic fashion. She's not formally trained but she has good instincts. Pardon me while I hang my hat on this hook."

He turned, removed his hat and reached out to hang it on a hook directly above his chair. Then he turned to face Nils and slowly lowered himself into the Peacock chair.

Nils could hear someone in the kitchen say, "he's here, take out his drink!" A couple of minutes later Melani emerged carrying a large tray with a half-filled crystal decanter and large cognac snifter. She sat the tray on the table next to the Peacock chair.

"Welcome Papa. I put your decanter and glass on the table in the same place as always. Shall I pour it for you?"

"Yes, please. It's the XO?"

"Yes, of course as always."

"I can tell the difference you know. I can smell it as well as taste it. By the way, Peni was late fetching me today. Ask your mother to talk to him. It's enough I employ her relatives in the car hire business but it's not acceptable for Peni to forget to fetch me on time."

"As you may have guessed by now Nils, I'm as blind as a bat. Late onset glaucoma. Wouldn't want to have the operation in this country and I don't travel anymore. I bet I'd be long gone before I went blind but I lost the bet."

"How's everything going with your new president? I wondered how long Americans would put up with becoming Socialists. Having seen how Sweden has destroyed initiative and its culture, I can tell you I have strong opinions. American parties are cargo cults. Everybody wants to get something for himself. It's all about me, me, me who I am and what I want. Blah, blah, blah. These kinds of people blame everyone else for their own failures and take no responsibility for themselves. They either want to steal everything or they want the government to take care of them from cradle to grave. To buy votes, the politicians will keep robbing the public purse to buy all the goodies for such loafers and put the country in hock. I lived here most of my life. I know how cargo cults work. Even today Solomon Islanders will line up outside Parliament to ask for handouts from their MPs. I'm Swedish but left Sweden because I could see what was coming a long time ago. It's not a paradise like some foreigners wish to think. What with the Muslim invasion and the everything goes social decline, it's as if Swedes have a death wish. Swedes are the ultimate in Socialist claptrap and self-deception. One day it'll blow sky high. Americans are headed in the same direction only slower."

"As far as the president goes," Nils responded, "let's wait and see. I understand why people voted for him. You are remarkably well informed and up-to-date."

"If I were trying to impress you I would say 'I've got my sources' and let you wonder. But it is no mystery, we live in a comfortable house in Honiara with internet and satellite television. Everything one could want for communication. I used to subscribe to news feeds from several news services but they just drove me crazy. The major US media on the internet blatantly censor news if the facts don't match their storylines. I get the audio edition of the Economist every week which is plenty liberal and anything I can't listen to Melani reads to me. She's a very well-informed young lady and an absolute sweetheart. Don't tell my other children but she's my favorite and not just because she's the youngest."

Pausing to savor a taste of his Cognac, Swede continued.

"Oh, I need to stop talking about all this political crap. I'll get too worked up and won't be able to sleep. What will you be doing during the rest of your time in the Solomons?"

"Kurt invited me to tag along with him on one of his demining trips to another island. He's going by chartered boat."

"Yeah, probably hired from Big Man Charters, another of my companies. My second son, Ismaeli, from the first wife runs that business. I can probably find out where you're going faster than you can. Melani," he shouted, "would you be so kind as to call Ismaeli and ask him where Kurt's charter is going?"

After a few minutes Melania came back into the dining where we were still talking politics.

"Oh, Papa are you talking this poor man's ear off with your political talk? Not everyone has such strong feelings as you. Anyway, I spoke with Ismaeli. He said Kurt chartered the boat to Makira. Since that is Mama's home island I think I'll tag along to visit the village and see grandma. I asked Ismaeli to check with Kurt since he is paying. Mama says she can handle things here without me since it is low season."

"Melani, you need a day off and a day away. Say hello to Mama's family. It's been years since I visited. There you go Nils. You'll have no better guide than Melani in all the world for Makira. She used to spend her school holidays there with her grandmother and has probably explored everywhere.

"Mr. Nils," Melani continued, "assuming Kurt doesn't mind. I'll meet you at the Mendana dock tomorrow at 0700. Once we get to Makira, I have something interesting to show you about an hour's hike through the bush. Be sure to bring long trousers and boots 'cause you'll not want to wear shorts and sandals in the bush."

"Melani, I am very glad you are going with us and very curious about what you want to show me in the bush. I'll need to wear long trousers and boots because it's difficult terrain for hiking?"

"Well, there is that," replied Melani smiling mischievously. "You'll find out tomorrow. Be careful on your drive back to Honiara. There will be cattle on the road and they don't have running lights. Good night."

At 0700 the next morning I walked onto the dock in front of the Mendana Hotel. There I met Kurt who introduced Swede's son, Ismaeli. They were loading Kurt's equipment into the twin engine open boat.

"I can see why you don't fly Kurt. That's a lot of gear."

"Yeah and a good morning to you. There's that plus where we're going there aren't any roads but lots of ocean. So, we go by boat. Ismaeli keeps my gear in a locker here so I don't have to schlep it back and forth every time I come here. I understand Melani is joining us. She's always good company. If I were younger I'd be very interested but I'm not young anymore and it wouldn't be mutual. She's too smart to get hooked up with me plus her father would ensure that I got disappeared. Nobody crosses the Swede and wins. He may be an old man and blind but Swede's too connected and knows too much. Here comes Melani. We'd better get underway. It's a long boat ride."

Hours later I remembered Kurt's warning about the rough ride. I expected chop but not the swells. I learned the hard way that small boats could indeed yaw as well as roll and pitch. After too many hours, we beached the boat at Kira Kira, the administrative center and checked into the Freshwinds Guesthouse. That evening we three chatted with Australian medical interns completing practicums at the Makira-Ulawa provincial hospital in Kira.

The next morning, I met Melani only to learn that Kurt and Ismaeli had already left with a Provincial Officer to a site about four hours down the coast where villagers had found an unexploded bomb from WWII.

"Mr. Nils, it's good to see you dressed in long trousers. Me too. I visited my relatives late yesterday evening. I have planned our day. First, we'll ride the bus for about two hours. Then we'll hike up the mountain for an hour to get to the site. Freshwinds will provide a picnic lunch. You can carry it because you are the man."

"Sounds very organized Melani. May I ask why the long trousers and what is at the site?"

"The long trousers are for the snakes and centipedes. You'll see why the site is interesting when we get there. Trust me! You'll understand."

After a bumpy, dusty ride, the bus left us on the side of the road in the middle of a lot of nowhere. For the first few minutes as we began our trek into the bush, Melani told me about her school vacations as a child, staying with her grandmother and exploring the bush with children from her grandmother's village. She described seeing green turtles lay eggs on the beach and about seeing a man wrestle sea crocodiles. Then after they forded a shallow river she sat on a fallen log and patted the space next to her.

"Let's take a break." She began. "We have a lot of climbing after this. It's easier if we follow the river into the swamp but that's where the malaria mosquitoes come from and they bite all the time not only when it's dark. More importantly, I want to talk about something serious. Nils, things are not as calm in the Solomons as they appear to a short-term tourist, someone like you. The Asians, mostly Chinese from Malaysia, are raping my country. A few years ago, there was a lot of resentment toward the Chinese Malaysian logging companies. There was a lot of violence directed mostly against local Chinese owned businesses. Most of those Chinese traders have been here for generations. Locals call the Chinese traders Wakus. Islanders confused them with the Asians from Malaysia who run the logging companies. The Malaysians are cutting and exporting ship loads of our logs. They pay big bribes to officials in Honiara to get permits. Traditional landowners are not consulted or given almost nothing. It has been going on since I was child. The loggers take our young girls and even the young boys into the camps and onto the ships. Some of them falsely marry very young girls by paying parents a bride price. The loggers abandon the girls and their children when they leave the Solomons. My people are simple and easily deceived. These companies are destroying our country, our culture, our traditions. It's happening not only here on Makira but throughout the country. My father does as much as he can to stop it but he is very old and weaker every day. We young people are taking a different and very indigenous approach. It's important good people outside the Solomons understand what's going on. Before we go any further though I have to ask you to swear on your life not to tell anyone."

CHAPTER SIX

SWEET MELANI AND THE HOLY MANA CULT

SOLOMON ISLANDS

"We're here Nils. This is the headquarters of the Holy Mana Cult. A coast watcher broadcast from this exact spot during the war. He was never caught. It's very well hidden and almost impossible to see from the air yet it has a view of almost the whole of Guadalcanal. What do you think?"

WHEN I HEARD MELANI SAY "swear on your life." I felt a shiver go up my spine.... What girlish secret could be so serious...? I decided none and cautioned myself to be less beguiled and more cautious of sweet Melani.

"You can rely on me to be discrete, Melani. I have been my entire career. I'm not a snitch. Of course, at this moment, I don't have the faintest idea of what we're talking about.

"Thank you. You'll find out as soon as we get there Nils. But I can tell you more as we climb the mountain. But being discrete, as you say, applies to what I say as well as to what you see."

For the next hour Melani and I fought our way through the shades of green, dense foliage which thinned as we gained elevation. All the while youthful Melani leapt over rocks, vines and cantered across open areas leaving me far behind.

"C'mon slow poke. We won't get there and back to the road before dark at this rate. We don't want to be here when it gets dark. Too much bad mojo."

"Melani, let's rest for a while. I'm not as young as you and not as fit so I'm not going to be as fast.

Where'd you learn the word mojo? Not in common usage in the Solomons I would think."

After they found a place to rest, Melani responded.

"Nils, you're not that old though I suppose Kurt is younger. He did OK hiking up here."

"You brought him up here too?"

"Of course. He supports our cause in all kinds of ways," she continued in an irritated tone. "By the way while it may seem like it to you, we're not exactly at the end of the earth here. We have satellite TV and internet most of the time. I keep learning. I know what mojo means."

"Sorry, I didn't mean to offend you."

"Men say that after they put a woman down with without thinking. You're forgiven."

"Thank you. It was thoughtless of me. Of course, you are well informed and very bright as well."

"Ok, you don't have to go overboard. Now I feel like you are patronizing me."

"Not at all. I'll just rest a while." I thought…I'll really never understand women.

"Nils, we are about halfway there so I might as well tell you more. You know about cargo cults in the Solomons and Vanuatu. We've started another. It doesn't focus on the white man bringing cargo like the cults that have grown and then faded since World War II. It focuses on the wealth we already have here and now, our natural resources, primarily tuna and forests. We call it the Holy Mana Cult. Solomon Islanders, my people, believe women hold the power of life. We call that power 'mana.' Men don't understand and are somewhat fearful of women's power over them. In the past there have been no women cult leaders. Ours is led by a woman and girls at least on the surface. Men are involved more on the active side. They are the secret army which no one sees. Since the authorities are paid off they do nothing. So, we decided to do something about it ourselves. The woman we call Holy Mama and the Chiefs' daughters go from village to village spreading word to create resistance to the raping of our forests, fisheries, girls and boys. It's the same simple message repeated time and again village by village."

"Wow, Melani I had no idea something like that is going on. It sounds like the Solomon's response is a version of a public relations campaign coupled with some kind of direct action."

"Yes, it is that and it is mostly unknown outside of the country but it is much more. We aim to shame our young men and leaders into action. That part is really growing. We'd better get going. I'll tell you more when we get there."

After nearly an hour more of exhausting bush whacking Melani and I arrived at a small clearing three quarters of the way up the mountain.

"We're here Nils. This is the headquarters of the Holy Mana Cult. A coast watcher broadcast from this exact spot during the war. He was never caught. It's very well hidden and almost impossible to see from the air yet it has a view of almost the whole of Guadalcanal. What do you think?"

I stopped hearing Melani as soon as I recognized what I was looking at. There in front of me covered with vines was a nearly intact World War II B-17 bomber.

"Melani, this is a B-17 Flying Fortress bomber. I can hardly believe it. It's got almost no damage."

Oh, the plane? Yeah, left over from the war. I suppose that's interesting to someone like you but what we care about are the caves."

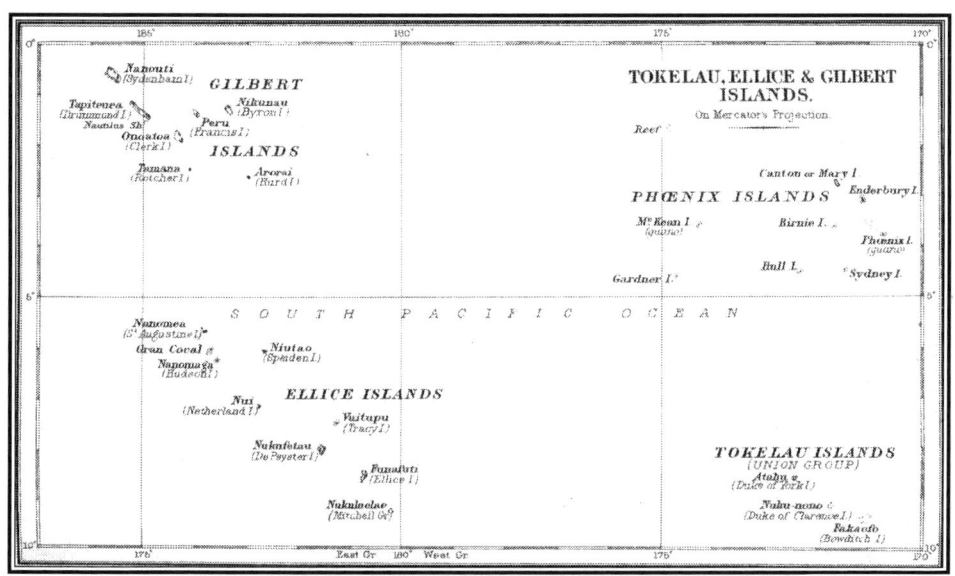

PART IV: KIRIBATI

Samoa a hundred years ago and long before, together with notes on the cults and customs of twenty-three other islands in the Pacific: Tokelau, Ellice & Gilbert Islands.
London. (1884).

Marines storm Tarawa. Gilbert Islands.
WO Obie Newcomb, Jr.; Marine Corps. Tarawa. (1943).

Japanese prisoners of war at Tarawa.
US Navy. Tarawa. (1943).

Japanese 14cm Guns on Tarawa.
US Navy. Tarawa. (1943).

CHAPTER SEVEN

WHITE SCARF PILOT AND SUBMERGED CAVE DWELLERS

KIRIBATI

I flew charters for Air America. Dropped bags of rice for the Hmong so they could fight instead of grow rice. Hauled all kinds of contraband as well. I named my company Celestial Products because I figured a lot of what I hauled sent folks heavenward. I just put the manifests in a satchel, took off and landed. I never, ever checked what we were hauling. Still don't.

HOURS EARLIER I HAD BOARDED an obscure, unscheduled Marshall Airlines flight from Honolulu to Kiribati via Majuro in the Marshall Islands. The airplane, a 1960s era British built Hawker-Siddeley HS-748, an ancient leftover, was more suited to ferrying cocaine from a derelict Central American airfield than flying passengers from Honolulu. My adventure started at check-in.

I approached a just opening Continental Airlines/Air Micronesia counter at six o'clock in the morning in Honolulu Airport.

"Excuse me. Could you tell me where the Air Marshall Islands check-in counter is please? I've looked everywhere and can't find it."

"Marshall Airlines?"

"Yes, That's right. Air Marshall Islands."

The Continental ticket clerk turned to her colleague. "Have you heard of an Air Marshall Islands check in desk? That's a new one on me."

"No, I haven't heard of it either. Wait a minute I'll look it up." He replied as he began keyboarding. "Nope, according to this, there is no such airline."

"No such airline?" I questioned. "You mean it doesn't show up in the computer? I have a ticket."

"It may not be an IATA member. Or maybe it's some kind of charter outfit. You may want to check down at the annex where they handle unscheduled and charter flights. They might know."

"OK. Where's that?

"Go out of the terminal, turn left and walk to the end of the departure access ramp. Go down the stairs until you get to ground level, then walk about 200 yards toward the UPS and FedEx hangars. You'll see a cyclone fence and a gate on your left and a small building marked Annex Terminal. Go in there and ask them. Good luck."

I dutifully did as I was told dragging my heavy luggage down the stairs and along a cyclone fence until I found the gate and a sign pointing to a corrugated roofed building marked 'Annex Terminal'. Once inside, I saw no one except for what looked like a pimply-faced high school boy taping up cardboard boxes marked 'airfreight.'

"Pardon me, hate to bother you, but I was told to come here to ask about a flight on Air Marshall Islands."

"Air Marshall Islands Airways? Yeah that's right. Is your name Torgerson?"

"Yes, I am Nils Torgerson and I am scheduled to fly on the Air Marshall Islands flight in about an hour. I have been looking for the check-in desk for more than an hour. Is this it?"

"Yup. You found us."

"Can you check me in? What about security? Is everyone else checked in already?"

"Yup. Everything else is already loaded. Just waiting for you. Got a gun or anything dangerous?"

"No."

Yup. Ok then. Security is all done. The pallets are mostly on board already. We usually only carry freight on the Honolulu to Majuro leg. Gimme your bag and I'll throw it on the cart. We can walk out to the plane together. I'll push the cart and you follow me. You're going all the way to Bonriki Airport in Kiribati?"

"Yes, your airline offers the most direct route. Mostly freight huh? How many passengers?"

"Oh, one: just you. We don't fly high or fast. But we get there ok. My uncle, Captain Muncie, is already on board. He's tying down cargo. We don't normally use the airline containers just pallets so he's got to net 'em and tie 'em down to the floor anchors. I'm Chet by the way."

"Good to meet you. You and your uncle handle the loading?"

"Oh yeah. Me and my uncle handle everything. You'll see."

Nils followed Chet who pushed the partially loaded luggage cart out of the small building's double doors onto the concrete apron in front of the Annex Terminal. Nils spotted a man driving a fork lift loading a freight pallet onto the turboprop airplane. Though Honolulu could not be described as cool, Captain Muncie was wearing a leather flight jacket and Captain's hat. Nils thought he only needed a white scarf to be a stereotypical pilot. The plane was ancient and sported the remnants of multiple airline insignia.

"There she is," Chet said pointing at the plane. "She's not pretty but she's a workhorse. I'll tell ya. She's perfect for those too short runways in the islands. My uncle used to fly off short runways in Vietnam and Laos for an outfit called Air America. He's got some stories I'll tell ya. Taught me how to fly too. But I just have co-pilot status. You might as well grab your carry-on and get aboard. There are sandwiches and soft drinks in the cooler at the back next to the toilet. Here's the safety announcement. Buckle your seat belt. There's a life jacket under your seat. I hope you enjoy the flight. It takes a while. That's it."

Within a few minutes they were at the end of the runway. I buckled my seatbelt when the powerful Rolls Royce engines sputtered as they revved to full power. I remembered what Chet said about the HS-748 being perfect for short and island coral runways. The takeoff was incredibly short.

After hours of airborne solitary confinement during which I looked at net covered cargo pallets between me and the pilots in the cockpit, I began to understand why I was the only passenger and why the flight to Kiribati via the Marshalls was so cheap.

Trying to be positive, I consoled myself by thinking about the sandwiches in the Styrofoam cooler and that I wouldn't have to wait in line to use the head. I stretched out on three seats and after what seemed like endless hours dozed off. The next thing I knew I was awakened by the screech of tires as the creaking plane sat down in Majuro.

Shortly after the plane taxied and came to a stop opposite a small warehouse with an 'Air Cargo' sign above a roll up garage door, Captain Muncie rolled a stairway up to the plane and opened the passenger door.

"Welcome to Majuro, affectionately known as the armpit of the Pacific by those who know her best. But that's only if you haven't been to Truk, the other armpit. You'll want to get out and stretch your legs. My nephew and I will be about an hour unloading most of the cargo. You'll be happy to know you'll have company on the flight down to Kiribati. We only have one pallet of freight but eight passengers so there'll be lots of room. Don't wander far though, we'll get underway as soon as we can. I want to get to Bonriki before the sun goes down. Being equatorial, that place gets dark fast. Plus, the guys from the airport authority, if you can call it that, often forget to turn on the runway lights. Once dark, it's a small bit of flat land to find in a lot of ocean. We'll have time to talk once we're up. Assuming we have a smooth flight, I'll crawl around the pallet and chat with you a while."

While I walked around within the fenced air cargo area I watched Captain Muncie unload the pallets while his nephew checked-in passengers. I wondered how the Captain could trust the pimply faced kid to fly the plane while he left the cockpit to chat. I made a mental note not to fly with any airline with a too good to be true fare in the future.

The seven other passengers and I sat on flimsy, white, plastic lawn chairs in the warehouse until someone noticed both Captain Muncie and pimply-faced Chet were on the plane. There was no official announcement but someone more experienced than me said.

"It's time to go. Let's get on the plane."

Once we were all seated, Chet crawled around the remaining cargo pallet and closed the aircraft door. He returned to the cockpit the same way. There was no announcement that take off was about to happen but the plane taxied to the end of the runway and we got the hint that something was about to happen. After the engines had made ominous coughing sounds and were up to full throttle, the plane lurched forward and started to take off. Most passengers took this as a signal to sit down and put on their seat belts. A couple of the passengers didn't feel the need for seat belts and pushed the seat backs in front of them forward and stretched out. A few minutes after takeoff a short, chubby young woman wearing flip flops, jeans and a faded orange T-shirt stood up in the front of the passenger section and turned to face the other seven passengers. I got the distinct impression she was talking only to me as she looked me in the eye as she spoke.

"Toilet's in the back. Sandwiches and soft drinks are in the Esky near the toilet."

Obviously not one to worry about a safety briefing about a water 'landing' nor about communication, she sat down and never spoke the rest of the flight.

As soon as the flight was at elevation Captain Muncie left the cockpit, leaving Chet to fly the plane. He crawled around the cargo pallet to chat.

"Is he OK up there alone?" I asked Captain Muncie as he sat down in the aisle seat next to me.

"Oh sure, he's Ok. It's on autopilot. Besides he needs the hours. What brings you down to Kiribati. Are you a World War II buff? Wanna see where the battle of Tarawa was fought? I can't think of another good reason to visit."

"No. I'm tracing some of Robert Louis Stevenson travels. How'd you pick this part of the world? Your nephew, Chet, said you used to fly in Southeast Asia for Air America."

"Yeah, all true. Before I answer your questions, I wanted to mention some weird things you should know about Kiribati and the i-Kiribati people. First, they live on these palm-frond-covered platform houses that offer little privacy and little shelter. So, they all make a point of 'not seeing' what other people do. The men get into fights easily and are good with knives. I-Kiribati fishermen are known to survive at sea in open boats for weeks. Lots of stories about that. Those that don't fish, which is most people, seem to work for government or not at all. Oh, and if you're a diver try to scuba down to the deep-water caves where they have evidence of human settlement. So much for this crap about sea levels rising. Hell, the sea levels have been rising forever. The coral keeps growing. We didn't start sea levels rising and we can't stop it. I started flying down here thirty years ago and even then, during king tides, the floors of the hotel were awash. You'll probably be staying at the Oceanside Hotel."

"Yes, in fact. That's right. The alternatives didn't sound very attractive."

"Neither is the Oceanside."

"Oh."

"Now to answer your questions. I picked this part of the world to fly in because it's peaceful, offers long distance flights and has little to no competition. Nobody wants these routes because you can't make much money. We do OK because we do everything. We don't have any overhead. The plane is my office and except for some agent fees we have no non-flight related expenses. If we can't make money we don't fly. It's that simple."

"Sounds like a well thought out business plan."

"I'm not a business person. I just like to fly. By the way, just so you know, I was not what those in the game will call 'a direct hire.' I was a contractor with my own airplane. I flew charters for Air America. Dropped bags of rice for the Hmong so they could fight instead of grow rice. Hauled all kinds of contraband as well. I named my company Celestial Products because I figured a lot of what I hauled sent folks heavenward. I just put the manifests in a satchel, took off and landed. I never, ever checked what we were hauling. Still don't. I figure if someone wants me to know they'll tell me. 'Can't tell you anything because I don't know anything.' That's always been my motto. Safest way to be."

"I suppose you're right. Better not to know huh?"

"Yup. You got that right. I better get back. I got to supervise Chet so he can get in his hours. Good talkin' to you."

After Captain Muncie left, I spent my hours straining to understand what his Micronesian I-Kiribati fellow passengers were saying but to no avail. Except for the occasional English word, I understood nothing. I whiled away my time looking at the endless expanse of ocean. I saw not a speck of land for the entire flight. Nearing Kiribati, the setting sun turned the sky yellow. The yellow light reflected off the sea like a million gold medallions as the HS-748 made its approach to the compacted coral runway at Bonriki Airport.

After the plane came to a stop in front of a garage sized, wooden, open shed an unseen Captain Muncie addressed his passengers from behind the pallets separating the seats from the cockpit.

"The Airport Authority staff will unload your bags and bring the stairs to the door in a few minutes. I've been advised as this is the only flight today, they're on a tea break. In the meantime, please gather your belongings."

CHAPTER EIGHT

FLIP FLOP PRESIDENT AND THE RUSSIANS ARE COMING

KIRIBATI

"Stranger things have happened. In fact, Kruchenkov offered the President a lot of money to purchase an island group from Kiribati and allow it to secede to create a new country. Then Kruchenkov intends to reestablish the Romanov Dynasty in a new and sovereign country."

EARLY THE NEXT MORNING Nils joined Captain Muncie at his table at the Oceanside Hotel just as he was finishing his breakfast.

"Good morning, Captain. Where's your co-pilot Chet?"

"Oh, hi Nils. Good to see ya. Chet's already at the airport handling check-in and loading. I'll join him right after I finish eating. We've got a routine. We fly down here Tuesdays and Thursdays then back to Honolulu via Majuro on Wednesdays and Fridays. That way I get to spend the weekends in Honolulu and work out of my hotel room on Mondays to set up freight and passengers for the week. Only bad part is overnighting in this fleabag twice a week. I bring a bottle of duty-free with me and sort of put myself in suspended animation the nights I'm here. By the way Chet mentioned that the flight from Nadi, Fiji, arrived. He said some Foreign Ministry Officials were on hand to greet the new American Ambassador, Jonathon Packard, and a couple of his staff. As I recall he's Ambassador not only to Fiji but also to Tonga, Samoa, Kiribati, and Tuvalu. He's probably here to present his credentials to the Kiribati 'Beretitenti' or President as we would say. Chet said Packard is in full formal dress monkey suit and looks as out of place as a mini-skirted streetwalker in church. Boy is that fancy pants diplomat in for a surprise. I see my ride is here. I gotta fly so to speak. See ya."

Captain Muncie excused himself just as a group of Americans entered the small dining room. Since Nils's table offered the only free chairs, three of them asked if they could join him while the fourth, obviously the over-dressed Ambassador Packard, demurred and headed off to his room.

"Good morning, thank you for sharing your table. This is Tom and Jeff. They are tourism consultants from the East-West Institute at the University of Hawaii. I'm Louie, the Economic Development guy, from Embassy Suva and you?"

"Oh, I'm Nils. I'm waiting for a flight to Abemama Atoll."

"Wow," Louie continued, "that's even more obscure than here. Coincidentally, we met a couple of United Nations, I should say WHO, doctors on the flight up here who are also headed to Abemama. Small world, huh? What do you recommend for breakfast?"

"Ahh, I don't think there's a choice. They give you eggs and bacon with toast and tea."

"Oh, OK. I'll order some scrambled eggs then."

"I don't know for sure but I think you get the eggs the way they give them to you. No special requests."

"Oh. I guess that's why they need Tom and Jeff's expertise." He replied, gesturing in their direction. They're tourism consultants from the East-West Center at the University of Hawaii."

Addressing the consultants Louie continued. "After breakfast you're free until our appointment with the Permanent Secretary of Finance tomorrow. You'll probably want to go over your notes and prepare for the meeting. Let's meet back here for lunch then develop a plan together for tomorrow's meeting. Tomorrow morning after breakfast we'll move to the lobby area to wait until the car from the Ministry arrives. We don't want to keep the Permanent Secretary waiting. He's got a lot on his plate. In addition to his day job as Permanent Secretary of Finance he's in charge of tourism, fisheries and God knows what else. In such a small place all the Permanent Secretaries have multiple portfolios. Most Ministers don't or can't do much except play politics so the Permsecs, for short, basically run the show. In the meantime, I'll be notetaker for the Ambo while he presents his credentials and has tea with the President. The Ambassador plans to fly out tomorrow afternoon. See you guys at lunch. Good to meet you Nils."

As I had nothing to do I wandered into the lobby area where Louie and Ambassador Packard were waiting in the Lobby. Before long a shimmering pear-colored Toyota Land Cruiser with a Kiribati coat-of-arms stenciled on the front door arrived. The Foreign Ministry Permanent Secretary, who had met them planeside, was sitting in the rear. Before the car came to a complete stop he sprang out of the car door and rushed toward the Oceanside Hotel's front door. He was dressed Australian style in an open necked shirt, shorts and knee length socks.

"Your Excellency, Ambassador Packard, the President is waiting anxiously to meet you. He has requested we keep this first meeting private and low key. We are going to his residence for morning tea."

The Permsec bowed and held open the car door motioning for Ambassador Packard to sit in the 'seat of honor' in the back. He ran around the rear of the vehicle and hopped in beside him. Louie sat next to the driver who turned up the air conditioning against the already torpid equatorial heat. Later Louie told me all about his morning in detail. According to Louie no one spoke during the drive. The Ambassador stared first at the expansive lagoon on their right and then at the ocean 100 feet to their left. The white coral road seemed to take up too much of the narrow strip of land. In places the land was so narrow that the road took almost all the space. They saw small grass platform houses on the ocean side of the road and signs for Westpac Bank, Punja's Tea Biscuits, Ocean Mackerel, Victoria Bitter and Foster's Beer. On the lagoon side they saw two Chinese Grocers and a half dozen rusting motorbikes along the way.

20 minutes later, the gleaming, pearl Toyota Land Cruiser stopped in front of a modest, one story wood frame house which had been painted a faded, unrecognizable color some years before. An unarmed policeman in a disheveled uniform and a dayglo orange baseball hat marked SWAT stood beside the entrance.

The Foreign Ministry Permsec spoke with as much officiousness as he could summon. "Your Excellency, Ambassador Packard, we are here for the presentation of your credentials."

As they exited the vehicle, the Permanent Secretary motioned for the Ambassador and Louie to go first. The policeman knocked on the door while the Permsec followed behind.

A youngish man wearing plastic, flip flop slippers, a T-shirt and striped Adidas sport shorts opened the door.

As if on cue Packard spoke first. "I am the United States Ambassador, William Packard, and we are here to meet the President."

"Yes," The man replied. "Please come into the parlor. I have set up the tea in there."

Ambassador Packard and Louie followed the man into the parlor and took seats next to a tea table set with three mugs, three plates and an opened can of Borden's sweetened, condensed milk. The table was positioned between the three simple rattan chairs all placed on a pandanus mat with a ragged fringe of red yarn.

The Foreign Ministry Permsec remained silent and moved away from the table to sit in a small chair near the door.

The man who had greeted them left the room and returned with a pot of hot tea and an unopened package of Punja Brand Tea Biscuits imported from Fiji.

"That is very kind of you," Ambassador Packard opined while pulling his shirt collar away from his red, sweaty neck which oozed over the top of his collar. "We are very much looking forward to presenting our credentials to the President."

"Oh certainly," the man replied while pouring three cups of hot tea. "But first I'll serve you some tea. The President has been looking forward to meeting you as well Ambassador."

"Excellent."

"Well now that we have our tea shall we begin?" The man said as he sat in the third chair.

After the Ambassador realized that the man opposite him was the President, he gave the President an original copy of his appointment certificate and his assignment cable. The two chit-chatted about 20 minutes. Then the Ambassador turned toward Louie.

"Louie, the President and I have a sensitive matter to discuss. We'd appreciate it if you could wait outside. We'll only be a couple of minutes." It was not a request. The Kiribati Permsec took his cue from the Ambassador and went outside with Louie.

True to his word, Ambassador Packard returned to the car a couple of minutes later. The Permsec wished them a pleasant journey and returned to the President's home.

Louie sat next to the Ambassador in the 'seat of honor' on their return drive to the hotel. The Ambassador turned toward Louie for the second time that day and spoke in a low voice so the driver could not hear.

"Louie, I didn't mean to be melodramatic by asking you to leave back there but I didn't know whether the President wanted any of his people to hear our conversation. I didn't know how to get his Permsec out of the room any other way."

"I understand, sir. Very gracious of you."

"Well I hope so. Now let me tell you for the first few minutes there I thought we were talking to some kind of houseboy. It shocked the bejesus out of me when the President sat in that chair. He's such a likeable, down-to-earth guy. I felt like a fool in this monkey suit. The matters we discussed are not classified but my conversation with the President is. You understand?"

"Yes, sir."

"I assume you've heard about this Russian businessman, Nikolai Kruchenkov, and his campaign to restore the Russian Royal Family, the Romanovs?"

"Yeah. Like that's going to happen. Absurd"

"Stranger things have happened. In fact, Kruchenkov offered the President a lot of money to purchase an island group from Kiribati and allow it to secede to create a new country. Then Kruchenkov intends to reestablish the Romanov Dynasty in a new and sovereign country."

"You're kidding right?"

"Nope, and we can't allow Kiribati to sell off part of the country even if the country will be awash in a few years. I heard they plan to start moving folks out of the country in 2020. There's a million and a half square miles of ocean that only Kiribati can lay any claim to. We don't want Russians of any kind mucking about in our lake. Who knows who Kruchenkov is fronting for. I delivered a formal Demarche from the Secretary. As a sweetener, we offered to help pay for two thousand acres Kiribati is buying in Fiji for resettlement of the i-Kiribati population. The President agreed. Remember it's classified . The conversation never happened."

CHAPTER NINE

HANKY PANKY IN THE OCEANSIDE HOTEL

KIRIBATI

Just as Tom finished speaking, the hotel guard came into the lobby from the lavatories adjusting his belt. Immediately behind him a small, barefoot woman, naked except for the small towel she held around her waist, dashed across the hotel lobby and ran out the front door stirring a cloud of dust as she ran.

EARLY THE NEXT MORNING Louie ran into Ambassador Packard after breakfast and agreed to brief him after the tourism consultants' meeting later that morning with the Ministry of Finance Permanent Secretary.

"Ok, Louie, I look forward to it. You get up here a lot more than I will so likely have a much better eye for the lay of the land. See you later. I won't be long."

The Ambassador hurried off to a meeting with the Kiribati Cabinet while Louie looked for his tourism consultants. He found them in the hotel lobby.

"Hi Louie," Jeff greeted him. "Tom and I are all prepared and look forward to meeting the Ministry of Finance Permsec. His name is Bokataki, right?"

"Yup."

"Well, let's get started with our initial impressions. I have a few observations already. Wanna hear 'em?"

"Sure," Louie replied. "Fire away."

"As I understand it, this is the best Western style hotel in the country and it is owned by the government, right?"

"Yes."

"If this is the best funded, top of the line hotel everything else must be down market. Here are my observations. What I thought was black Australian vegemite on the table at breakfast this morning was actually labeled apple jelly. It had turned black because the date stamp on the bottom of the little packet expired five years ago. The breakfast was like what I would expect in a badly run youth hostel. The towels in my bathroom had holes in them and the pillows smelled musty. The sheets on the bed are torn and stained, my room was not cleaned and the drapes won't fully close. The fire extinguisher outside my room has no hose. Just sitting here waiting for the car I can see thousands of beer cans in the lagoon next to the bar. It looks as if hotel customers just toss their empties into the lagoon from the bar. The staff in this place appear to have little to no training. Management controls and maintenance appear to be nonexistent. Those are just my impressions from the few hours I have been here. I hate to think about the reservation and accounting systems. It is like going back in time."

"Jeff, of course, what you observed is exactly why the country needs tourism consultants like you guys. Given your combined experience in management and marketing, you and Tom could transform this place. Am I being too optimistic?"

Tom chimed in. "Kiribati does have surf, sand and sun but so do a lot of places. That isn't enough anymore. Some locations just have potential and always will. You can't sell potential. Kiribati may remain one of those potential locations unless we can determine some factors that define a niche market. By the way what is that muffled screaming sound coming from the lavatories behind the bar? I noticed several local men going in there. Is there some kind of construction going on? It's not even eight o'clock. Do they start work that early? The two women at the reception desk don't seem to take any notice. I just saw the Security Guard go in there as well. That sound has been going on for about 15 minutes."

Just as Tom finished speaking, the hotel guard came into the lobby from the lavatories adjusting his belt. Immediately behind him a small, barefoot woman, naked except for the small towel she held around her waist, dashed across the hotel lobby and ran out the front door stirring a cloud of dust as she ran. The guard sat in his chair by the front door and didn't look up. One woman at reception looked at the counter top and appeared oblivious to what had just happened. The other turned her back so as not to see what was happening. Louie walked over to the reception desk and spoke to the receptionists behind the counter.

"You have to call the police. What just went on in the hotel lavatory can't be allowed. And your guard, who is supposed to keep order, evidently was involved. That is shameless. You have to call the police."

"Oh mister, we cannot call the police," the older of the two replied. "People will get in trouble. In Kiribati we cannot get involved with each other's problems."

"I understand your Chief of Police is English. He's not i-Kiribati. I think he'd want to know. This is a government owned hotel. You have a responsibility to report it."

The two, short, stocky receptionists wearing identical black t-shirts both tied back their hair with matching pink ribbons, looked first at each other, second at the countertop, then at their shoes. They said nothing. At that moment a white Land Cruiser arrived at the front door.

Louie turned to face the two consultants.

"Gentlemen, our ride has arrived. We can discuss this whole incident with Permanent Secretary Bokataki. It looks like nothing more is going to happen here in any case. Let's go."

Shaking the thick dust from their shoes they got into the Land Cruiser. A plaque attached to the front door of the car stated "Gift from the Japan International Cooperation Agency (JICA)." The JICA funded deluxe Land Cruiser stirred huge clouds of dust as it made its way along the coral and dirt road to the Ministry of Finance housed in a dilapidated unpainted, two story wooden building.

"Here we are at the Ministry of Finance," Louie began. "We might as well get this meeting started. I'll start off by telling him what just happened at the hotel. Perhaps the Permsec will respond and deal effectively with what just happened there."

The three sat in the waiting area in the Ministry of Finance while one of the Permanent Secretary's assistants, a young woman in a faded pink T-Shirt, and a red hibiscus flower design wrap around skirt served them tea. After ten minutes they were ushered into the Permsec's Office. Secretary Bokataki wore a purple Polo shirt, shorts and sat behind an enormous, dust covered desk with four telephones, each a different color. The fan in an ancient air conditioner made an irritating, never ceasing clink, clink, clink sound as it rotated.

"Mr. Secretary, it's a pleasure to see you again," Louie began. "Thank you for taking the time to meet with us. As you will recall from our earlier communication, we are here for eight days to prepare a National Tourism Development Feasibility Study for Kiribati. These two gentlemen are Jeff Mullins and Tom Erickson from the East West Center at the University of Hawaii. But before we begin I want to tell you about an incident we just witnessed at the Oceanside Hotel."

After Louie explained what had happened at the hotel only 30 minutes earlier, he asked the Permsec for a comment.

"Thank you for that explanation. Let me ask you just one question. What direction did the woman go after she ran out of the hotel?"

"Well, I think she ran to the left," Louie replied. "But what does that have to do with what I just described to you?"

"Everything. She was probably from the mental hospital and wanted it." The Permsec responded.

"It happened in the ladies' restroom in the lobby of your government-owned hotel. Your staff evidently are complicit, at a minimum, and perhaps directly involved. You mean to say that the incident I witnessed officially doesn't matter because the woman is mentally ill?"

"Yes."

"Mr. Secretary, I think I understand the situation here perfectly now." Louie said as he faced the consultants giving them a look of disbelief. "I'll leave the consultants here to chat with you for the remainder of the meeting. I have to go back to the hotel to meet with our Ambassador about his flight. He has just presented his credentials to your President and has met with cabinet. Thank you for providing the car and for making time for us to meet with you. I'll send the car back to pick up the consultants within the hour."

Louie got into the scorching hot JICA funded Land Cruiser. He fastened his seat belt, closed his eyelids and rolled his eyes. He enjoyed feeling the icy cold blast of air from the Land Cruiser's air conditioning as he thought about various ways to describe what had happened to Ambassador Packard. After he arrived at the Oceanside hotel, he met briefly with the Ambassador and described the incident for a second time and repeated the Permsec's comments.

"Ambassador, you're leaving today but the last plane out for a week is tomorrow. I'm booking the consultants and myself on that flight. We were scheduled to stay a week longer but given the incident and the response, I've decided this culture; this country is a long way from being ready for tourism. How can they screw it up so badly?"

"Louie, I don't have to remind you that it's their country. I guess they have a right to 'screw it up,' as you would say, if they want to."

"Maybe so," Louie replied somewhat chagrined. "Maybe we can assist them some other way but I'm not going to conduct a national tourism feasibility study. It would be a total waste. That's not going to happen. Not on my watch."

CHAPTER TEN

LOSING SIGHT AND WHERE'S THE MAN? SEPPUKU

KIRIBATI

"Listen! I was awakened in the night by some rustling outside my cabin. It was like someone walking through dried leaves. I went back to sleep. Next thing I know, I was awakened again by someone in my bed next to me feeling my chest. I couldn't see anything in the darkness and was about to scream when I heard a female voice say. 'Where's the man?'"

A N INFECTIOUS CONJUNCTIVITIS EPIDEMIC was spreading throughout Kiribati, an island country comprised of atolls hardly above sea level that spreads across more than a million square miles of the Pacific Ocean from the Line Islands south of Hawaii to more than 100 miles south of the capital of Tarawa, Kiribati, across the Bay from Betio where the Japanese and American forces fought the Battle of Tarawa in November of 1943.

The World Health Organization dispatched two ophthalmologists to find out what was causing the conjunctivitis epidemic and recommend how to end it. Following their arrival at Bairiki, Tarawa, they checked into the government owned Oceanside Hotel.

After three days of fact finding in Tarawa and nearby atolls, they took a couple of days break and went across the harbor to the island of Betio to see the war wreckage remaining from WWII. Their guide told them about the course of the battle and the U.S. Navy miscalculation of the depth of the water in the lagoon which resulted in the grounding of landing craft far out on the beach. After they walked to the ocean side of the island the guide stopped in front of what was left of gun emplacements.

"As we just saw U.S. Marines fought their way across open beach for half a mile on the lagoon side of the island. The beach was named Red Beach due to all the blood spilt to capture Betio. The Japanese still lost the battle because of their own miscalculation. Even though Betio is only two miles long, the Japanese were sure the Americans would attack from the oceanside. So, the Japanese positioned their big guns to point out to sea. The guns were the same ones the Japanese captured from Singapore where the British were also sure an invasion would only come from the sea. The guns could not swivel. They were fixed in one direction. You won't see that in the history books."

The next morning, the two doctors and an elderly Japanese, Yoshiaki Koutoku, flew to an airport on Abemama about 90 miles southeast. B-24 bombers flew out of the World War II airport to bomb Japanese in the Marshall Islands. There they checked into the coconut and pandanus palm thatched Robert Louis Stevenson Resort on the deep-water lagoon. At the resort over lunch, they met Nils Torgerson who was retracing Robert Louis Stevenson south seas travels. After meeting district health officials, they established a base at the hospital in Kariatebike and went in different directions to conduct their epidemiology surveys.

In the meantime, Nils was learning all he could about the locals' attitudes about Stevenson who had lived in Abemama for several months in 1889 and about their infamous, some would say tyrant chief, Tem Binoka, who Stevenson mentioned in his account of voyages on the schooner Equator in his book "In the South Seas".

Later that evening after the two doctors had finished their field work, they met on the resort verandah to compare their findings.

"Susan, I know you met Nils but not Mr. Koutoku. He's here on some family matter. That's all I know."

"I look forward to meeting him. Doctor Guy, after I finished my work in the villages I returned to the hospital to examine one of our little patients. She's about three years old. Both her eyes are swollen shut and inflamed like golf balls. Her mother, her own eyes red from crying, sat on her daughter's bed. The little girl, who must be in considerable discomfort, reached for her mother, hugged her mother's head and patted her mother to comfort her. It was so touching. I don't know if you have reached the same conclusion I have Doctor but I have a hunch about the cause of the conjunctivitis as well as a solution to the outbreak. Tomorrow I will seek to verify the behavior I think is causing the conjunctivitis. Tomorrow, I will share my findings. Good night."

Shortly after sunrise Doctors Guy Rath and Susan Milkovich walked the dozen paces from their separate beach cabins and sat across the breakfast table from each other on the covered verandah at the edge of the lagoon. Nils joined them few minutes later, but before he did Doctor Milkovich asked her colleague about the night before.

"Guy, something totally unexpected but also interesting happened to me during the night. But before I tell you about it I want to ask you a question. Did anything disturb your sleep last night?"

"No, nothing disturbed me. I slept like a baby. I guess it's the ocean air. It must be soporific."

"Listen! I was awakened in the night by some rustling outside my cabin. It was like someone walking through dried leaves. I went back to sleep. Next thing I know, I was awakened again by someone in my bed next to me feeling my chest. I couldn't see anything in the darkness and was about to scream when I heard a female voice say, 'Where's the man?' Within seconds the person, whoever she is was gone."

"Of course she was looking for me," her colleague replied. "Do you think she was looking for Nils or that Japanese guy? Nils is retired and the Japanese chap has to be in his 80s. No. She was definitely looking for me. I'm still in my prime. Those two guys are over the hill. Hm... hm... hm...."

"Oh, you compliment yourself doctor. What a narcissist you are. Aren't we scheduled to go to the last atoll today? Isn't that our last field visit before we catch a flight back to civilization?"

"Yes, and both Nils and the Japanese guy are going with us. Nils is interested in the Robert Louis Stevenson connection to Abemama. The Japanese guy said his father lived there for two years. I don't know more than that. We can ask him on the way."

Dr. Guy sat next to Mr. Koutoku on their way to the atoll. While driving across the causeway he asked. "So, you're here to visit family?"

"In a way," Koutoku replied. "I am here to visit my father's burial site."

"Oh sorry. It's a sad time for you. Did he want to be buried here since he lived here before?"

"I will tell you more after we arrive."

As Guy had been itching to ask his colleague sitting in front of him about her conclusions since the previous evening when she said she had a hunch about what was causing the conjunctivitis epidemic, he blurted out what he was thinking.

"Okay Susan my curiosity is just killing me. What's your hunch about what's causing the epidemic?"

"I thought you'd never ask," she answered smiling from ear to ear." There's a pattern to the infections. It runs in families starting with the older children and then gets passed to the younger children. This pattern is repeated in nearly every family. My hunch is the children are trading t-shirts. The young ones wear the t-shirts after the older ones have finished wearing them. The t-shirts are not washed. When the infected children pull the t-shirts over their eyes they then transfer the conjunctivitis to the t-shirts and thus on to the younger children. If we merely stopped allowing children to pass their unwashed t-shirts to their siblings the epidemic will be over. I'm 99% sure at this point but want to confirm that pattern today in the last sentinel villages."

When they arrived at the final atoll in the chain of islands they had visited, the two doctors walked beside Nils and Mr. Koutoku into the village.

"You asked if my father asked to be buried here." Koutoku said quietly. "No. He had no choice in the matter. I was born early in the war just after my father was conscripted into the Japanese Imperial Army. When the war ended we didn't know what happened to him or where he served. He wasn't allowed to tell us where he was posted. I just knew my father didn't come back home. I grew up never knowing my father. I made it through university, became a salary man at Mitsubishi and worked in international marketing. That's where I polished my English language skills.

We kept trying to find out about my father. It was like putting together pieces of a puzzle. Our war time ministries kept good records but many records were destroyed, lost or deliberately 'misplaced' after the war. Finally, I put together enough pieces to know he was sent to Abemama as part of a small detachment to slow the advance of Allied forces in Kiribati. We think he was here from late 1941 until Allied forces took Abemama in late 1943."

"All of the Japanese soldiers stationed here died here. Allied accounts say the last 25 soldiers dug their own graves in the coral sand, lay down in them and committed suicide. There were no officers in Abemama and no romantic suicides of warriors disemboweling themselves with swords. These were all enlisted men deemed not worthy of swords. These soldiers used what they had. Some shot themselves through their chins. In Japan, at the time, surrendering was seen as dishonorable. Death was preferable to dishonor. We Japanese call that sacrificial suicide Seppuku. We have several words for suicide. Japanese used to think there was honor in that but no more.

I do not know if he was killed or was among those who killed themselves. But that matters little. I am here to see where my father died. His body was never recovered. I have come here to be as close to him as I'll ever be and to honor his memory."

When I was down beside the sea
A wooden spade they gave to me
To dig the sandy shore
My holes were empty like a cup
In every hole the sea came up
Till it could come no more.

—*Robert Louis Stevenson*

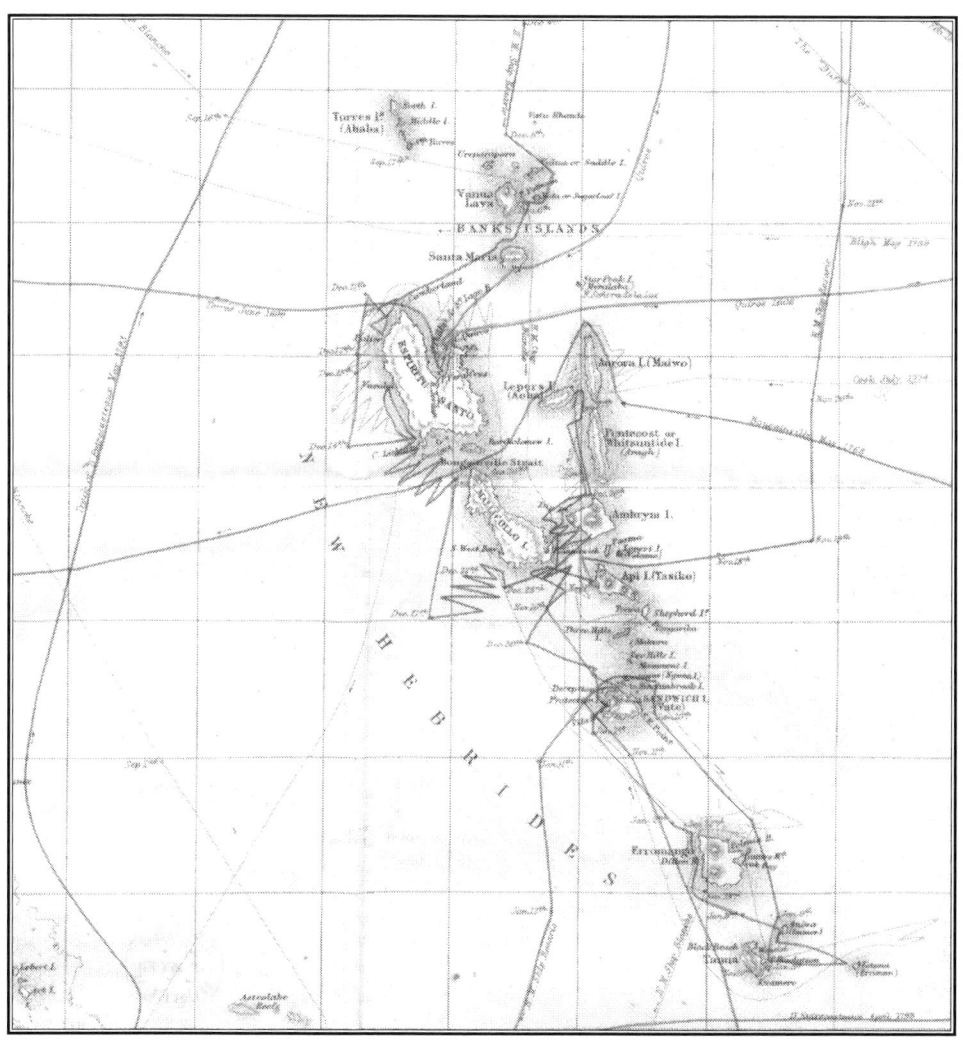

PART V: VANUATU
The Cruise of the "Rosario" amongst the New Hebrides and Santa Cruz Islands
Markham, Albert Hastings - Sir, K.C.B. London (1873).

View in the island of Tanna.
Drawn from nature W. Hodges. Engrav'd by W. Woollett. No. XXIX. Published Febry. 1st, 1777 by Wm. Strahan, New Street, Shoe Lane & Thos. Cadell, in the Strand, London.

Man of the island of Tanna.
Drawn from nature by W. Hodges. Engrav'd by J. Basire. No. XXVI. Published Febry. 1st, 1777 by Wm. Strahan in New Street, Shoe Lane & Thos. Cadell in the Strand, London.

The landing at Erramanga, one of the New Hebrides.
Painted by W. Hodges. Engraved by J.K. Sherwin. No. LXII. Published Feby. 1st, 1777, Wm. Strahan, New Street, Shoe Lane & Thos. Cadell, in the Strand, London.

CHAPTER ELEVEN

JUNGLE BUNGEE AND MR. AND MRS. QUEEN

VANUATU

Dateline: Pentecost, New Hebrides, February, 1974.

He also felt queasy but not because of the jump. He had jumped dozens of times before. But he had always jumped in the right season when the vines were springy, elastic and strong. He had never jumped out of season. No one did.

THOUGH A SPANISH EXPEDITION sighted the island in 1606, it was the Frenchman, Louis Antoine de Bougainville, who named it the Island of Pentecost because he sighted it on the Day of Pentecost, May 22, 1768. The French maintained a continuing role together with the British in the colony that the English explorer, Captain James Cook, named the New Hebrides in 1774. The name remained until the Coconut War and independence in 1980 when the newly formed country declared itself Vanuatu.

The empire building days were history. The British Empire swagger of the Raj had become the sclerotic shuffle of a weak, old man. The golden days of the colonial service were gone. The sun was indeed setting on the British Empire. Nonetheless, in 1974 Queen Elizabeth and her Consort, Prince Phillip, were traveling the colonies to showcase the Union Jack. One more time British pomp and circumstance would hold sway for many in the colonies no less in the least and one of the smallest the New Hebrides in the Pacific Islands. During this last hurrah tour the Queen and the Prince still commanded the devotion of their subjects and the romantic notions of every mesmerized young girl in the colonies.

18-year-old Meli Bani had been a land diver since he was five even before he was circumcised. He remembered the pride he felt the first time he was allowed to jump. As far back as anyone could remember he was the youngest boy allowed to participate in the annual fertility of the soil ritual. On his first jump, the older jumpers taught him how to measure the length of the vines he tied to his feet. On that jump he only went halfway up the 100-foot Nangol Adi tower. The older boys made sure his vines were short and flexible. It was sometime before he would learn to carefully choose liana vines, measure carefully and know just how far the vines would stretch so that he could touch the ground with his hair and shoulders to "grace the ground" ensuring maximum fertility for the yam harvest. According to tradition, the yam harvest would be better, the plants taller and stronger if more jumpers could grace the ground just as he had learned to do. As he matured, he enjoyed the power of his masculinity and the ensuing accolades from the young women who could never know his secret thrill when jumping. For it was forbidden for a woman to land dive.

The taboo for women and girls to land dive or climb the towers was rooted in native mythology. Given the preeminence of custom land ownership as the basis of wealth it had been practice for as long as anyone could remember for girls as young as ten to be forced to live with her future husband's family. Most often the girls had no knowledge that a certain man in the household was to be her husband until her late teens. One bright young girl came to realize that she was betrothed to a middle-aged man whom she hated. After multiple, futile attempts to run away she devised a plan to deceive her husband-to-be by climbing an immense banyan tree. She taunted the man that she would commit suicide rather than marry him. She tied air roots to her ankles which would stop her land dive just short of the ground and, still taunting her betrothed, dove earthward. The banyan tree's many air roots hid her from view after her jump. Her distraught fiancé had climbed high into the same banyan tree to save her but after seeing her jump and assuming her dead he jumped to his death. She then unfastened her constraints and climbed to the ground. Free at last.

The District Agent had told Meli's Village Chief that Governor General Sir Anton Clive-Smith insisted the village of Bunyan on Pentecost and the jump be included in the Queen's February 1974 tour to showcase the New Hebrides. The Bunyan Chief had not mentioned that Pentecost jumpers only jump from March to June. During the preceding months heavy rains ensured the vines would be green with just the right elasticity. He did not mention it and the date was set. Now it had become a matter of pride and honor for Bunyan and indeed for all of the New Hebrides.

Close to his home in Bunyan Village Meli sat on a senile, fallen coconut tree near where the river runs into the sea. As he ran his fingers through his reddish, blond hair he glanced at the river where he glimpsed a fifteen-foot-long sea crocodile hunting for sleeping turtles for lunch. Meli then glanced at the rocks on the shore where he saw a Coconut Crab deposit her eggs into the sea. He watched another, immense, Coconut Crab rip open a coconut husk, crack the shell and claw out the meat. He thought about catching the lobster like crab for dinner but decided to do so another day. He knew his mother was already preparing him her best dinner of boiled taro root, fresh ferns in coconut milk, and blue parrot fish steamed with lemon grass to strengthen him for his jump the next morning. He thought how much he loved his family and how honored he was to be chosen to be jumper for Mr. and Mrs. Queen.

Meanwhile in Port Vila, the capital, the British Colonial Governor General, Sir Anton Clive-Smith, explained to his royal guests just how the New Hebrides unique government came to be and how it worked.

"Your Royal Highness and Prince Phillip, the New Hebrides is what we call a condominium. It is unique in that since 1906 it has been governed conjointly by two powers, Great Britain and France. The origin of this somewhat odd arrangement is a triumph of diplomacy. The French run their schools and public services and we run ours. We divvy up the government ministries, such as they are, and meet jointly to coordinate and avoid duplication. It works quite well from the powers point of view. Good cooperation and all that but I'm afraid to say the locals jokingly call the country a pandemonium rather than a condominium. There are rumblings of an independence movement amongst the Anglophones but given the slow pace of change in the Pacific Islands who is to say when such a thing may happen."

"Oh, goodness," The Queen replied. "That must make everything very complicated. Isn't it confusing sometimes? I mean for the natives."

"Oh, well. At this point, given the general level of education and development outside Port Vila, very few natives actually interact with government only with Missions, medical centers, police and provincial agents. It's a system mostly geared to European residents. You'll see what I mean about the level of development when we go to Pentecost tomorrow. You may be in for a bit of a shock."

At that moment in Pentecost, 18-year-old Meli Bani kicked mud as he walked to inspect the Nangol Adi tower. He knew what was expected of him tomorrow. It was a great honor to jump for the people he knew as Mr. and Mrs. Queen from England. For him it was a once in a lifetime opportunity. He also felt queasy but not because of the jump. He had jumped dozens of times before. But he had always jumped in the right season when the vines were springy, elastic and strong. He had never jumped out of season. No one did. Nearing the tower, he looked up at the tree trunk and vine structure he had climbed so many times before and thought about tomorrow's jump. As he did so he felt a shiver. He dismissed the feeling. He knew he could jump from the highest point on any tower and soar to the earth and climb up again to soar earthward time and again. He smiled as he remembered when as a boy his phallocrypt came off during a jump. Everyone laughed and he joined them but, embarrassed, ran off into the bushes to make everything right again.

When the sun rose the next morning Meli was already awake. He was excited, thrilled and honored. He put on his wide belt, his phallocrypt and stretched his arm around to his back to tuck decorative grass into his belt. His parents and sister, Racheli, walked with him to the tower where a large crowd had gathered. He could see the honored guests sitting on a raised platform facing the tower. They dressed in white and wore funny looking hats. Meli had never met a foreigner before. At the appointed moment, Meli climbed the tower. As was his habit he did not look at the ground. He had no need. He knew all eyes were upon him. He looked up at the sky. As he climbed higher and higher he began to feel the sensation, a shiver of elation. He would spread wide his arms and fly. He was not to know that the warm days would change the elasticity of the vines tied around his ankles for the out-of-season jump. He could not know that this would be his last land dive. That he would be the first jumper to die. He would never know that his act of self-sacrifice to entertain the British Royals would make the news around the world in conjunction with Queen Elizabeth's tour. And he could not know that decades later young people around the world would imitate his jump for the Queen that day on the Island of Pentecost. But these future young people would not know about him nor jump with vines to grace the ground for better yam crops. With nylon cords tied to their ankles they jump off bridges, mountains and towers merely for the thrill.

I climbed to the high tower
And stretched out my arms
As if to soar like a bird
I looked up to the sky
Not down to ground
And knew that I could fly

—Meli Bani, Bunyan, Pentecost, New Hebrides, November, 1974

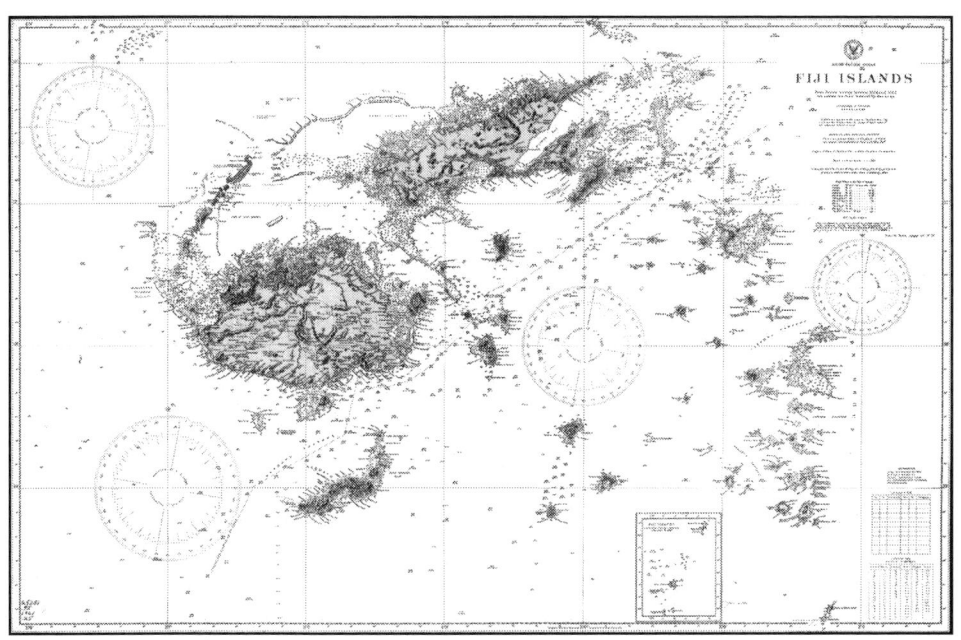

PART VI: FIJI
South Pacific Ocean. Fiji Islands
United States. (1914).

Club dance, Feejee.
J. Drayton. Endg. by Rawdon, Wright & Hatch (Philadelphia: Lea & Blanchard. 1845)

Queen of Rewa.
Drawn by A.T. Agate. Welch & Walter sc. (Philadelphia: Lea & Blanchard. 1845)

Tanoa, King of Ambau.
Drawn by A.T. Agate. Engd. by Rawdon, Wright & Hatch (Philadelphia: Lea & Blanchard. 1845)

CHAPTER TWELVE

MOOCHERS, THIEVES AND ISLAND DETECTIVES

FIJI

The overlord rooster who reigns over a kingdom of five hens began crowing. He set off other roosters nearby. Awakened by the rooster's cacophony some dogs started barking. Both roosters and dogs must have had some kind of code for false morning alarm as soon they all went silent in unison.

BEFORE RETURNING TO FIJI I made a life changing visit to China to meet a woman I had been corresponding with for more than a year. After we met face-to-face in Xishuangbanna, Yunnan, China, I was not just smitten but love-struck. I was gone. We visited back and forth between her home and mine for about a year then we married. The Little Woman and I formed a perfect team.

Back in Fiji the cell phone alarm went off this morning at 4:15 in the adjoining guesthouse room. Given the thin, plywood walls separating the guestrooms everyone else could hear the alarm as well. The three guys who had been staying in the room for the past two weeks installing a nearby cell phone tower groaned almost in unison. One by one they clomped down the long hallway to the one toilet.

At four in the morning, I hear every sound even with those little foam earplugs stuck in my ears. Next door there was a hubbub at the neighbors, whom I call the Ramshackle Neighbors. The overlord rooster who reigns over a kingdom of five hens began crowing. He set off other roosters nearby. Awakened by the rooster's cacophony some dogs started barking. Both roosters and dogs must have had some kind of code for false morning alarm as soon they all went silent in unison.

Later, the early risers began cooking in the communal kitchen where the previous evening I saw they had made a curry. About 5:00 o'clock their taxi arrived and they dragged their bags along the hallway making as much noise as they could and left, ostensibly to depart on the early morning ferry. We managed to go back to sleep.

About 7:00 we were awakened by loud talking and laughing from the room. I muttered to myself. "Oh no the roommates from hell have returned." But that was not what I found. Having decided a cup of coffee would be the best thing I shuffled down the hallway to the kitchen and noted there were seven different people milling about. All were well-dressed and prosperous looking. As I entered the kitchen I saw the oldest woman from the group picking through other guests' food packages. Thinking that odd, I asked. "Have you just checked in?"

The woman replied," I am looking for the sugar."

Thinking most about coffee, I made a cup and sat on the veranda looking at the garden. The seven made tea with copious amounts of sugar, ate four or five loaves of bread, used the toilets, left their dirty dishes, grabbed their bags and walked away. We never saw them again.

Just before lunch Kinman, the local detective, was sitting on the veranda, smiling and writing on his notepad. Elinoa summoned him earlier this morning when she discovered her chicken missing from the freezer. Kinman complained that he has to cope with double the number of criminal complaints this month over last month.

It was a wonder he can keep up, according to what Elinoa said later, since "that means the number of official complaints has gone from one to two." Kinman was posted to our little village from the international airport and sugarcane town, Nadi, on the main island, Viti Levu. Nadi residents tend think of their town as a sophisticated, up-market tourist attraction. That is because most of them have never been anywhere else. Tourists come there because of the airport. Then they leave for the island resorts and the beaches. They don't come to Fiji for Nadi itself. Back to Kinman, the town detective. My brother from another island far away calls his small town's policeman, one bullet Bob. Our local Sherlock Holmes, Kinman, has neither a bullet nor a gun. He also has no patrol car, no motorcycle, no uniform and no schedule. He does carry a notepad in which he takes exhaustive notes about his cases, both of them.

According to Kinman, local thieves are not greedy for cash, electronics or cell phones so much as they seek a quick on-site snack and what we will call euphemistically, take-away food.

"In fact," Kinman explained while sitting at the table opposite me, "food theft is the most common complaint the police receive. Thieves sneak into kitchens and open refrigerators to see what is already cooked for the next day. Often, they will snack before leaving."

"In fact," Kinman explained while sitting at the table opposite me, "food theft is the most common complaint the police receive. Thieves sneak into kitchens and open refrigerators to see what is already cooked for the next day. Often, they will snack before leaving."

I think they quickly would skulk (I haven't seen them but imagine them to skulk) away with the loot. Kinman calls our crime "the case of the missing chicken" (and prawns for the record). The chicken was intended for dinner but we ate vegetarian mock sausages (green banana, oatmeal and flour) to honor his memory. Not the thief's memory but the chicken's. Mosese, Elinoa's son-in-law, who drives her taxi and squats in her modest house boasted' "If he comes again, I'll cut him." I suspect the chicken thieve is one of the mysterious seven and their ring leader, the well-dressed woman, from earlier that morning.

As I write this it is evening. In the distance I hear pounding on the lali (log drum) reminding the locals of mid-week worship. Earlier in the day, while the children began the long and arduous task of clearing out 30 years of accumulated trash from under the house to earn money for Christmas, the neighbor's dog was having one helluva time killing the other neighbor's chicken which was stupid enough to wander into the dog's fenced territory. He was a bold young rooster but will never become an old bold rooster.

The hysterical screams coming from under the house from the children watching the dog try to kill the chicken were interspersed by Hindi screams from the neighbor to his dog to stop, stop killing that chicken. All of those screams were periodically interrupted by the Little Woman providing me regular directives from the kitchen where she was boiling water. Often when I didn't immediately respond, I would hear some Chinese invective she would say just loud enough so I could hear. I determined water boils very slowly as half an hour later she returned to our room wondering why I hadn't performed the assigned tasks.

Earlier it was starting out to be a lovely morning. The monster truck with a lifting mechanism for 20-foot containers finally pulled out of the neighboring driveway up the hill only to be replaced by a full-sized bus a few minutes later. How I sometimes long for the environmental sterility of some restrictive zoning covenants. But I guess trucks and buses are better than the crematorium in another neighborhood nearby.

Earlier in the week, the neighbor's younger brother suddenly appeared as usual just in time for lunch. After lunch he borrowed her taxi and disappeared for a week to the other side of the island. I noticed his return yesterday evening as he was explaining how someone had broken the left front light, dented the door and ripped off the front license plate in three separate incidents. He promised to pay her this morning but disappeared shortly after breakfast. Given his past exploits, I doubt we'll see him for a while.

A young goat appeared sometime during the night and was tethered in the grassy field across the road. During my morning walk I assumed at first glance that it was a Nanny goat. Only later in the day did I learn that it was no Nanny goat but a well-endowed Billy goat. Given the upcoming holiday season, I wonder how long he will be around.

While overhearing the flotsam and jetsam of the day's gossip, I heard about an 86-year-old charged with raping a 17- year-old school girl. This is only one day after another octogenarian was charged with a similar offense. While tragic and regrettable incidents, somewhere in the dark recesses of my mind, I wondered about the diet of these senior citizens. Could it be papaya, coconuts, even bitter gourd?

Speaking of bitter gourd, The Little Woman keeps trying to trick me into eating it. Now while I think of myself as a reasonable guy, I no longer swallow her explanation that bitter gourd will taste better after the third mouthful. It doesn't taste good no matter how many times I eat it. Yesterday after saying try this she pushed some deep-fried morsel into my mouth. You guessed it. I trusted her and she once again contrived to deceive me into eating some bitter gourd made by the neighbor. It tasted just like bitter gourd. Bitter.

There are, the Little Woman attests, many uses for bitter gourd. After burning up the internet with frantic distress calls to her friends in China, they confirmed her conviction that a poultice of bitter gourd leaves could cure her prickly heat.

Now if a baby's nappy (diaper to you Americans) rash is like a camp fire of the nether regions, the little woman's prickly heat was a major forest fire. I was dispatched to the market where she had arranged for delivery of bitter gourd leaves from a fruit and vegetable vendor who knows another vendor who has a friend who just happens to have a supply of bitter gourd leaves. Five dollars later I brought home the leaves. I was told I paid too much. In defense my motto is 'no price is too high' to cure the Little Woman. She made up a foul-smelling poultice and rubbed it over her forest fire, ahem, I mean prickly rash. A couple of days later, it really did begin to heal. We won't mention my provision of medicated powder a couple of days earlier. I dare you to eat even one mouthful of bitter gourd.

CHAPTER THIRTEEN

THE GUESTHOUSE: CAUGHT RED-HANDED, NO ROOM AT THE INN

FIJI

"I think if they had gone back this late at night only the sharks would have a Merry Christmas. That is so foolish. They just don't think. But I had to help them. What could I do? It's Christmas Eve. I can't turn them away."

I CAN ADMIT WHEN I'M WRONG. It is not something that happens often in my opinion but it does increase in frequency when the Little Woman is around to point out my mistakes. The Chicken Thief was not one of the Mysterious Seven at all. I offer an apology to their memory for suspecting them of stealing the chicken (and shrimp) from the freezer in the always unlocked kitchen. This Christmas Eve morning, the real thief struck again at 2:30. Alisha, Elinoa's daughter, heard a sound in the kitchen. She went to investigate to find the culprit with his head in the freezer. The culprit explained that he had a Fijian friend, James, in Room Five who told him to get some food from the freezer. Too bad for the thief, the guy in Room five wasn't Fijian or James but me. But it was a quick and ingenious lie thought up in a flash by a slow-witted thief. Alisha quickly grabbed the nearby Sasa (Fijian broom) and kept the thief at bay by threatening to whack him while other family members called the police.

Alisha, who knew the thief, was berating him. "Masood, you know this house. My parents took you in when you were only eight years old after your mother abandoned you. They fed you, gave you clothes and put a roof over your head. Remember how you stole $50 when you were 14 and then ran away. Now you are stealing again. This is how you repay them. Shame, shame, shame on you. You turned 18 only four days ago. Remember how we used to get a birthday cake for you? Now you are 18-years-old. You are no more a child. Now you are going to go to jail."

When Elinoa appeared in front of him, Masood began to cry.

"Mum, please forgive me. I'm sorry. I'm sorry. I'm sorry. Don't call the police they will put me in jail. I'm sorry so sorry. I won't steal again. I'm so sorry."

Elinoa listened and looked sad. Obviously out of patience she replied, "you stole from us at least twice before and again last week. You are already doing it again. But it's true you won't do it again because you'll be in jail."

"But Mum," he began.

"Don't but Mum me Masood. Now you're in for it. Now you'll get it. When you arrive in jail the other prisoners, they'll give you a real beating. And that's probably not all."

A policeman patrolling nearby appeared from the roadside. He called Elinoa by name and exclaimed "I got a call on my radio to come here about a thief. So, it's him is it? I saw him earlier with another boy down by the hot springs."

As the policeman questioned him, Masood told him the other boy down by the hot springs had told him to steal some food from the guesthouse.

"I come here because I know there's food. Like before it's unlocked. Elinoa trusts people."

The policeman grasped the young man to take him to jail and smacked him on the back of the head.

"You stupid. You really stupid."

As the two walked out of the garden into the darkness on their way to the jail. Alisha questioned me. "Why didn't you come out before?

Shamefaced, I replied, "I thought you and Mosese were having a fight and I didn't want to interfere."

"Mosese and I don't fight like that. When I scream, it is because I want help," she replied. "Besides, Mosese slept through everything. He's a very sound sleeper." I thought back to Mosese's empty boast the first time they discovered food missing about a week earlier, "I'll cut him next time."

Later in the evening that Christmas Eve, Alisha learned that the night shift policeman had released Masood. She was livid. "They released him. Why? Why would they do that?"

Having seen a public service announcement on Fiji One, the local television station, requesting citizens to telephone the Deputy Police Commissioner if they suspected the police were not doing their job properly, Alisha found the number she had written down and telephoned the number. The Deputy Commissioner in Suva answered the phone himself. Alisha was surprised that it really worked. She told the Commissioner about the release of the repeat offender who had just been released from remand (custody) for an earlier offense. She also told him that Masood threatened her. The Deputy Commissioner was most responsive and told her he would order the case to be dealt with this very evening. He also advised her he would order the Provincial Commander and Labasa Police to oversee the matter. Alisha's conversation with the Deputy Commissioner must have made a difference because a police officer and Kinman, the detective, walked into the garden 15 minutes later.

"Our superintendent ordered us to come here and said the matter was urgent. What is the problem?"

"What is the problem?" Alisha replied. "You don't remember the theft you came to investigate about a week ago. We told you we suspected Masood. You told us it couldn't be him because no one would be stupid enough to have a snack at the scene of the theft. Last night at 2:30 in the morning, I caught him in the act of stealing all the food for our Christmas dinner. He had everything packed in plastic bags but was making himself a cup of tea. The night patrolman came and took him to jail. We told the patrolman that Masood had already been arrested a couple of weeks ago and was released from remand just a few days ago for that. Since then he's robbed us twice. We told the officer we would definitely press charges. Then earlier this evening a friend told us they saw Masood downtown. Why was he released?"

Detective Kinman was obviously rattled. "Well, I understand the night officer let him go because your husband told him to let the boy off with a warning."

"Mosese would never say that. He wanted Masood in jail more than anyone. The patrolman shouldn't have let him out and is trying to save his own arse with that lame excuse. What are you two going to do about it?"

Fearing his superintendent and possible further repercussions from the Deputy Police Commissioner in Suva, the detective replied, "We are going to hunt him down like a pig."

This morning at breakfast, Alisha mentioned to me she heard from a friend who works at police station that Masood, the 18-year-old multiple offender, chicken (and prawn) thief also didn't show up in court on the scheduled date for his hearing earlier in the week.

"Kinman, the old poofda, said he will 'hunt him down like a pig'."

I dropped my fork. "Alisha, you mean Kinman, the detective, is gay?"

"Of course, he's a poofda. What did you think?" Alisha replied.

"Well I didn't think anything."

"Didn't you notice how overly friendly he was?"

"Well I did think he was very, very casual while investigating Masood's theft. But I thought that was because he was from Rotuma. I mean they are very friendly people."

"They are not that friendly."

"Oh. I didn't know."

"That means he likes you."

"Me? Oh, you must be joking. Me? How could he like me? I'm not like that you know?"

"A poofda?"

"Yeah, I'm not gay."

"Everybody knows that."

Visibly relieved, I said, "Oh good." In an uncharacteristically politically correct moment I added "not that I have anything bad to say about them."

"No?" Alisha asked.

"No, of course not. They are that way. I'm not." Thinking it best to say nothing more, I changed the subject. At least I thought I had. "Oh, speaking of colorful characters, have you ever noticed that very tall large woman with the flamenco dancer outfits and huge hats walking around town?"

"Yes, of course. His name is Aunt Vili."

"His name?"

"Yes, He's a Fijian poofda and probably the most famous one in town. There are lots of them. No one hassles them but he likes to dress up and have people look at him. Certainly, Aunt Vili has been around longest. He runs the beauty shop downtown past the Copra Shed on the other side of the street."

"He's a transvestite?"

"Well, he wears women's clothes. He's often quite fashionable. He also has long nails and beautiful soft skin. He does massage if you are interested. I think he does house sitting for expatriate families. He must be reliable because they ask for him year after year."

I queried. "My goodness. Savusavu has more than its share of characters and unusual people doesn't it?"

"Well, I don't know." Alisha replied. "It all seems kind of normal for us. Some people are just different. And some people are the same. What can we say? At least different makes things interesting and relieves the sameness and boredom. You know it can be awfully the same here every day. That's why a lot of young people leave for Suva, the big city, and never come back. They'll visit at Christmas time or school holidays but they don't come back to live. I mean there are so few opportunities here. Mosese and I are thinking of leaving for New Zealand. He can drive big trucks you know. There are a lot of openings for experienced drivers in New Zealand."

"Yes," I replied. "There are not many job opportunities here unless you want to process copra, work for the government, drive a taxi or go fishing."

"That's about it. The Indians employ their relatives in their shops. They don't trust anyone else. There are a few jobs in the resorts but they pay peanuts."

"Yeah, by the way if Masood is on the run, where do you think he went?"

"Likely he went to the village where he grew up or maybe Labasa or Suva."

Surprised I asked. "Village? But he is Indian and a Muslim. What do you mean village? He's not Fijian."

"He's not Fijian obviously. But his crazy mother gave him to a woman in the village to care for when he was a baby. His mother came and took him from the woman when he was eight. He always thought she kidnapped him from the village and his real family because to him they were family. That's all he knew. Besides, his mother had so many kids from so many different men I don't think she raised any of them. Her family kicked her out when she was just a teenager. Indians will do that. They'll just kick you out and part company.

The Fijians will never do that. They live with the guilt. They'll say 'bring them to us in the village.' They are not necessarily more kind or understanding. Fijians beat kids and abuse wives and parents too. I know because I am half Fijian and half Indian and speak both languages. I look mostly Indian but look at my hair. It's a dead giveaway. My mother is obviously Fijian and my father was Indian. I have a foot in both cultures. I see the strength and the weakness in both. Neither is perfect. Neither is all wrong.

Poor Masood. He's really mixed up. He's all Indian but culturally Fijian. Talk about internal conflict."

About an hour later the policeman phoned Alisha to report that they had found Masood drinking with his buddies in town. He reported they arrested him again and took him to jail.

Just as I thought it safe to go back to bed and that all the drama of the last 24 hours was over, several sets of eyes peered into the garden from behind the roadside hibiscus hedge.

Elinoa saw them first. "Oh look. There are some people from the Bush. They peep like that before they enter. I remember from when I was a child in the village. They peep."

Elinoa walked out to the roadside to meet the visitors from the bush. Though none of us back at the house could see after she returned to the house Elinoa told us that at the moment she got to the roadside a dual cab pickup drove by. In an instant the driver slammed on his brakes to avoid hitting one of the youngest children who darted across the road directly in front of the vehicle.

"The father went over to the child and slapped her on the back of the head. These people from the bush don't know much about cars. Likely it is that little girl's first trip outside the village. There are only horses there. No roads and no cars. They just don't know.

"They have come by boat from Kabalau all the way out at the end of the bay before it opens into the sea. They came to Savusavu to do Christmas shopping. There are two adults and eight children. But their engine won't start and they are stuck here for the night. I think I'll let them sleep in the family room for $60."

Since the Little Woman and I occupied the adjoining room I said selfishly, "but won't that room be a little small for ten people. There are only four beds."

"Oh, several of the children are very small. They can share. They are from the bush. That's normal for them. But you are right they may disturb you."

Feeling guilty, I replied, "well yes. You are too generous Elinoa."

Always the peacemaker, Elinoa replied. "I have to help them though. It is Christmas Eve. I'll let them sleep across the road in the church. I have a key. We'll take over some pillows and sleeping pads. They can talk all they want there."

I felt sheepish and relieved at the same moment. "Yeah, that's a good solution."

After the family was settled into the church Elinoa joined me and the Little Woman on the veranda.

"I don't know what those people are thinking," She said. "Bringing eight young children and two adults in a small open boat with a defective engine across miles of open water is dangerous. They must have traveled two hours across the bay. I think if they had gone back this late at night only the sharks would have a Merry Christmas. That is so foolish. They just don't think. But I had to help them. What could I do? It's Christmas Eve. I can't turn them away."

Feeling even more sheepish, I said, "Yes, it is Christmas. You did the right thing. Good night." I went back to bed.

CHAPTER FOURTEEN

THE BAND SAW MASSACRE AND RITE OF PASSAGE

FIJI

This story describes a common rite of passage circumcision procedure performed on boys entering primary school. While tastefully presented you may want to skip this story if you would find it unsettling. Circumcision has become a much more controversial subject in many places but not in Fiji. The story is included because it is a daily part of life and helps the reader understand cultural norms and pressures.

BLOOD RAN DOWN THE WALLS and splattered the ground at the back of the Ramshackle Neighbor's house. He was at it again. The high-pitched whine of the ancient commercial band saw he had salvaged from a long-closed butcher shop periodically lugged down as he guided the goat carcass through the dull blades.

"I can make these steaks double or triple thickness if you want. You want them thin like Morris Hedstrom (MH) sells them or do you want them thick?"

"Oh, it doesn't matter," the customer replied. "I am mostly giving the meat away. I sacrificed this goat for our Muslim big Eid celebration which we call Eid Al-Adha. You Christians celebrate Ibrahim being willing to sacrifice his son and Muslims do the same to celebrate the willingness of Ibrahim to sacrifice his son Ishmael for Allah by sacrificing a sheep, goat, cow or camel. We're supposed to give most of it to charity and friends. They don't have to be Muslims. In fact, I am going to pay you for your work but also will offer you some meat for your family if you will accept."

"Sure, we will accept," the Ramshackle Neighbor said with a smile, "happy to help you out. You won't have so much to carry that way. Where did you get this goat and how much did you pay for it?"

"We paid three hundred dollars for it from Montfort Technical. The boys there raised it. It's about five kilometers out the Labasa road. You know it?"

"Sure, the training school for boys run by those Catholic Brothers. I know because I'm Catholic."

"You, I thought almost all Fijians Methodist."

"My family come here from the Solomons long time ago to make copra. My great grandfather was indentured laborer. He's buried somewhere on the Waikei Estate. That's the plantation on Nakawa Bay side eh? I'm not Fijian but I am Catholic. That's why I know about the brothers. They train a lot of boys who need help eh? I learned how to cut meat at the old Montfort Boys Town on Viti Levu. I used to work for MH here in Savusavu you know. That's before they closed down the meat market. That's where I got this saw. It was junk. I got it for free and fixed it."

"Oh, so you really know it. If you were trained on Viti Levu how did you end up back here in Savusavu?"

"I met this girl from here you see. She part Solomon too. One thing led to another. You know what I mean? And there she is inside the house. We got five now. Two boys and three girls."

"Yeah, I understand. I'm going in the shade under the mango tree to have a smoke and let you finish your work. I see you got some other customer just drove up."

"Yeah, he's the one with all the frozen opakapaka (snapper) I got to cut up into steaks for his restaurant. Enjoy your smoke. I be finished in about ten minutes, eh?"

Just down the road from the Ramshackle Neighbors, six-year-old Josefa lay naked and shivering on Doctor Khan's stainless-steel treatment table in the air-conditioned surgery.

"Josefa, Doctor Khan began, "I'm Doctor Khan. Do you know why you are here?'

"Yes," Josefa answered, "because my Grandma Elinoa said the doctor had to do something so I could go to school."

"Well Josefa, you are finishing Kindy class and going to go to the first class in primary school soon I hear. That is why we are doing this little procedure. Lots of boys in Fiji do this before they enter school you know." "Yeah, that is what Grandma Elinoa told me," he answered, his voice wobbly, "she said I need to come here and you need to do something all boys do here. What is it?"

"You don't need to worry about that at all Josefa," the doctor said reassuringly, "you just lie here, put your head on the pillow and relax." Noticing his small patient's shivers, he said. "Are you cold? Do you want a blanket?"

"No, I am not very cold. I am just shaking because I am afraid."

"Well your grandmother wants you to do this so you will be the same as other boys and not be looked upon as different. She wants you to do this so you will fit in."

A nurse came into the room with a syringe in her hand to assist.

"What is that?" Josefa timidly asked.

"Oh, you don't need to worry about that, Josefa. Pay no attention. The nurse is just coming in to help me." Josefa watched Dr. Khan inspect a scalpel from the sterilized instrument tray.

Wide-eyed he blurted out. "What is that for?"

"Nothing. You don't need to worry about it. The nurse is going to fasten your legs into those holders on either side of the table so you will be more comfortable."

As soon as the nurse finished strapping Josefa's legs into the stirrups she gently grasped Josefa's arms and held them across Josefa's chest.

"Josefa I'm going to give you something to help you feel less."

As the nurse held Josefa's arms across his small chest, Dr. Khan quickly injected lidocaine multiple times in a circle around the base of Josefa's penis. Josefa screamed. It wasn't a small scream nor a mad scream but a blood curdling scream of unmitigated horror. Everyone inside the clinic and in the surrounding neighborhood could hear.

"That hurts," Josefa screamed. "Oh Jesus, what are you doing? What are you doing down there?

The Ramshackle Neighbor turned off his saw to hear what was going on, the other children stopped shouting and playing games to listen. Grandma Elinoa, in the doctor's waiting room, knew what was going on and smiled uncomfortably.

"Ok, Josefa, that is finished. Now we will wait a few minutes. You understand?"

Josef, obviously relieved, said, "Doctor, is that it? Are you finished? Is it over?

"That's it for now Josefa and the last part won't hurt much at all. You can relax."

Josefa lay there looking at the ceiling, counting the flies on the window, shivering from the blast of the unfamiliar air conditioning. After a few minutes he heard Dr. Khan whisper to his nurse.

"Ok let's finish this off. This is taking too much time. I've got another client with a serious problem in the waiting room."

The nurse replied. "Do you think the lidocaine has had time to take full effect?"

"Sure. Its fast. Let me show you." Dr. Khan pinched Josefa's foreskin with an artery forceps. You see no reaction. If there is any sensation, we should wait a further five to seven minutes and test again. We are almost good to go. The procedure will be over with so quickly. I'll just grasp the clamp firmly, position it and cut. It'll be over in a few seconds. Then I'll do the sutures."

"What are you doing now?" Josefa screamed. "That hurts too. Oh Jesus, Oh Jesus, is it over? Oh Jesus."

"There we go. It's all finished Josefa. Now we just need a couple more stitches and you will be just like the other boys. There we go." He said after he had finished the sutures. "I'll just put a bandage on the little cut. You can take it off tomorrow. You will be sore down there for a few days. It is better you wear a sulu (wrap around skirt) and no shorts until you are not sore down there anymore. Do you understand? Now, I'm going to help you down from the table and the nurse will take you out to your grandmother in the waiting room. She'll also give you some sweet lollies because you were such a good patient. See you later Josefa."

The nurse helped Josefa down from the table while the doctor joked and prepared for the next patient. Legs akimbo, Josefa walked slowly to his grandmother in the waiting room taking great care to keep his legs apart.

"Elinoa," the nurse began, "Josefa will be sore down there for a few days. The doctor said it is better he wears a sulu and no shorts for a few days. Here is some Paracetamol to give him."

"I'll make sure he is comfortable, Elinoa responded, I've gone through this several times before with my other boys. Will the doctor stop by the house later?"

As promised, later that evening Dr. Khan stopped by to see Elinoa to check on Josefa.

"Bula, Elinoa," Dr. Khan said as he came near the open front door.

"Bula, Doctor Khan, please come in and have a cup of tea."

"Thank you but I don't have time. I've got to check on two other patients yet this evening. "

"Are you sure?"

"Yes, yes, how is my little patient? Any excessive bleeding or problem."

"Not as far as I know. Josefa," she called, "can you come in here for a minute please?'

As soon as Josefa entered the room and saw the doctor in the doorway, he hid behind his grandmother.

"Nana, ask that man to go. I don't like that man."

"Josefa don't be like that. He came to check on you. Are you bleeding down there? Do you want him to look?"

"Nana, ask that man to go. I don't want him to look. Ask him to go, please Nana."

With a mischievous grin Dr. Kahn added. "A lot of my young boy patients have that same attitude. I can never figure out why. Glad to know he is feisty and walking. I'll be going. See you sometime at the clinic."

After little Josefa's ordeal and about the time Elinoa gave him some ice cream the Little Woman returned from shopping at the Chinese store on the waterfront. She told me a strange tale.

"I had a really upsetting conversation with a rather strange girl," the Little Woman began. "I was sitting at one of the picnic tables down at the Savusavu Yacht Club to rest. You know the table under the tree?"

"Yes, I know it, the one closest to the water under the tree." I replied.

"Yes, that one. It's right by the water. Well this Solomon Island girl walked up the bank from the water and sat right next to me. I know she was from the Solomons because she had that striking, natural, blond hair and that's how she started the conversation."

"Oh, OK. Tell me more."

"As she sat down next to me she said, 'Hi, I'm from Solomons. Call me Lizzy. We left eight days ago and sailed here in that little boat.' She pointed at a small sail boat that couldn't have been more than about 16 feet long."

"Wow," I said. "that's an awfully small boat to take into the open ocean."

"Yes, it is small but Robin says it's seaworthy. Robin is my new boyfriend. He bought the boat from some American man who sailed it from some place called Port Townsend in America to Honiara in the Solomons. But he not want to sail it anymore after he come to Honiara. So, Robin bought it.'"Then she started to play with her cell phone and tried to dial a couple of numbers but got no answer. That is when it started to get weird."

"Weird? What do you mean?" I responded.

She said to me, "don't tell Robin I have a phone. He not know I have this phone. He not want me to have one. He keep my other phone."

"I told her, 'I don't know who Robin is but if I do meet him I won't tell him you have a phone. Why doesn't he want you to have a phone?"

Hesitantly, she began to tell me her story.

"I'm 19 and Robin is my new boyfriend but my parents not know I am with him. He was selling lots of phones to the shops in Honiara. That is how I met him. He came into the Chinaman's shop with big box of cell phones. The Chinaman was my old boyfriend. He has shop and also export sea slugs to Hong Kong. I live with him four years. He bought me from my parents when I was 15. But after I meet Robin, the Chinaman said I can leave if I want. So, I went on the sailboat with Robin. But Robin thinks I want to leave him. I have Aunt here and am trying to contact her."

"Do you want to leave him?" I asked. "I mean you can if you want to. You are not his possession. Do you need some help of some kind? Do you know anyone else here?"

"No," she replied. "I don't know anyone else here. I'm OK I guess. It's just that sometimes I don't want to be with him. You know. I'm grown up. I don't have to do what he tells me to do. I guess I shouldn't have told you all this. Maybe I should have told my parents. I mean the Chinaman did say I can go."

"That is very strange," I responded. "First, her parents sold her when she was 15. It's hard to believe that sort of thing can still happen. Then she runs away from the guy who bought her and then sets off across the ocean in a tiny sailboat with some guy she just met. Yeah, I would say that is bizarre. Is she in some kind of trouble? She's over eighteen and can make her own decisions but what she is doing is pretty bizarre. She doesn't sound simple but she appears to be troubled."

"Yes," the Little Woman answered. "I am sorry for her. I went back after lunch and the boat was gone."

CHAPTER FIFTEEN

VIRGIN OIL, BLACK MAGIC, YOU CHEAT ME!

FIJI

Ishmaeli peeled off his rugby jersey and his sleeveless undershirt exposing his bare chest. After pouring what he called "virgin oil" into the palm of his left hand, he announced. "Now I am ready. Are you ready for hard massage? Praise the God. You're going to see God through my hands eh?"

THE LITTLE WOMAN, ALWAYS SEEKING THE best for me, began asking the neighbors who could provide a good massage to alleviate my back and leg pain. One neighbor recommended his young niece who had been through what he described as "extensive" formal training course to become a masseuse. Not one to be easily bamboozled the Little Woman interviewed the young lady. She learned that Shelly, not yet 18, had completed only three weeks of training with a local masseuse and charged F$35 per hour, double the going rate in the community. When the Little Woman asked for references the young lady admitted she hadn't actually done any massages. The Little Woman thanked Shelly for her time and politely mentioned to the neighbor that she might be willing to pay once to test Shelly's skills but only at a fair price.

The Little Woman resumed her search and soon found a well recommended masseur.

When he showed up the afternoon that first day, we quickly learned his mother called him Ishmaeli (unfortunately pronounced "ish smelly"). His mother hoped, according to Ishmaeli, that he would become the village's first professional man.

"She hoped and prayed I would become a doctor, lawyer or a teacher." He said. "I did better. I became a healer. Praise God. God knows how many people I have healed with one hour of my excellent massage. Now we do massage eh?"

Ishmaeli peeled off his rugby jersey and his sleeveless undershirt exposing his bare chest. After pouring what he called "virgin oil" into the palm of his left hand, he announced. "Now I am ready. Are you ready for hard massage? Praise the God. You're going to see God through my hands eh?"

I began to ponder exactly how that would work but instead lay on my stomach cupping my hands to hold my nose above the mattress. Feeling I was in charge I announced. "Yes, I am ready. I have two things to mention. One, please be gentle with my left leg. Two, please don't use too much coconut oil."

Back to the massage at hand, I braced for the pain to come. Ishmacli poured a small swimming pool of virgin oil into the small of my back and began to gently knead. I felt no pain but did feel rivulets of virgin oil flowing down my sides onto the sheets and mattress.

"Do you know my village? It is the third village past the big church village at the end of Savusavu Bay. We have thousands of acres of Mataqali (tribal) land. You can come and invest with us and show us what we can do with the land. What do you think eh?" Without waiting for an answer Ishmaeli continued. "You know some people here still practice black magic?"

I began to wonder if Ishmaeli practiced black magic but all such thoughts instantly vanished when Ishmaeli's massive hands slid down my back and across my left buttock to massage my leg. The pain began. As Ishmaeli clasped my leg it was as if the earlier request to "please be gentle with my left leg," had never been heard or said.

After I turned on to my back, I expected a perfunctory massage of the head and legs like so many previous massages I had experienced; however, Ishmaeli had his own style. Suddenly, without warning and in a single movement, Ishmaeli made his move. He jumped on the bed, straddled me and began to massage my head. Afterwards, when I discussed Ishmaeli's massage style with the Little Woman as a kind of after action debrief and critique, I could only describe the straddle position as an extraordinarily awkward moment.

While massaging the Little Woman, Ishmaeli experienced his own awkward moment. The Little Woman broke into uncontrollable laughter when, unexpectedly, Ishmaeli made the same move when massaging her. Her laughter immediately unnerved Ishmaeli who jumped off the bed onto the floor in a single move. Later, after he resumed and was massaging her sides she again began laughing.

Ishmaeli couldn't handle that either. He asked. "Did I do something wrong?"

The Little Woman smiled and said, that's OK. Don't worry."

Obviously rattled, Ishmaeli massaged the Little Woman for the remaining minutes with what could only be called great consternation and copious amounts of virgin oil.

After he was paid Ishmaeli drifted out the door as I wafted into a deep sleep. Strictly in the sense of massage, Ishmaeli had his way with my body and worked magic.

Three weeks later, Ishmaeli, arrived uncharacteristically late for our evening massage. He staggered through the door supporting himself on both sides of the door jamb as he moved.

"Gooddd Ebeninggg," he began, "here for massshaaage, massshaaage for you, massshaaage for madam. Massshaaage."

I thought, Ishmaeli is very, very drunk. How do I humor him? And how do I get rid of him?

"Hello, Ishmaeli. It looks like you have been enjoying yourself early this Saturday. Are you sure you can do a massage? You may...."

Ishmaeli cut me off, "Of courrrrssse I can dooo massshaaage. Nooo problemmm." He said as he fell to the floor into a sitting position and crossed his legs as if his action was intended.

"We go. I shhtart massshaaage."

Thinking it best not to argue, I reluctantly walked to the bedroom followed by 125 kilograms of drunken 50-year-old also known as Ishmaeli.

Ishmaeli slopped large puddles of virgin oil onto my back. It dribbled onto the sheets below. He placed his massive hands on my back and began to knead quietly for several minutes.

"You shheee. I can massshaaage. No problemmm. You my daddy. I love you daddy. You come to my village. We have plenty land, plenty land. You can shooow us what to doooo. I know you got plenty money. We got plenty land. I no con man. No con. Speak truth. God knows. You can invest in our agriculture. I plannnn banana, dalo (taro), vudi (short fat banana similar to plantain) yaqona (kava) in our village. Wat you thin?"

I could only think about drunken Ishmaeli's strong hands massaging my foot and chose my words carefully. "Ishmaeli, I think I would be happy to visit your village but cannot decide about an agriculture project now. Tell me more about your village."

"You know. Is third village passss big church village at the end of bay. We have thousannns of acres of lan. You commm home and shooow, shooow us whaaa we can doooo with the lan. We have haaa spring in river. You sit in haaa water gooood for you. Natural healing. God's healing. You commm to village I make sure you live to 100. We have secrets too. You commm home. We shooow you."

I felt Ishmaeli's hands twist my back. It hurt. I was being man-handled. The alcohol had dulled Ishmaeli's sense of touch.

"Oh, be gentler Ishmaeli! You are very strong tonight."

"Oh shorrry, shorry. I do sofff. I do sofff."

I turned over to try to bring the massage to an end more quickly. I thought about the Little Woman and how Ishmaeli's strong planter hands could actually hurt her. I hoped she would feign sleep so I would have an excuse to send Ishmaeli home after only one massage.

"Ishmaeli," I began, "the Little Woman is asleep. I don't want to wake her. So, it is better if you go after one massage tonight. I'll pay you the money and ask you to come back next Friday not Saturday but Friday. OK?"

I was relieved when Ishmaeli answered.

"You shaaay I commm next Friday?"

"Yes, that is good for today," I answered handing him the $20. "You come next Friday. OK?"

"OK. I go naauu an' commm Friday. You like massshaaage?"

"It was very strong, Ishmaeli. You are very strong."

"Thank you. Vinaka, (Thank you). Vinaka vaka levu (Thank you very much). Friday at 7:00?

Friday at 7:00. Correct. Bye."

"Ni sa moce (Goodbye)."

I sighed and went back into the bedroom where the Little Woman was sitting bolt upright in bed.

"Nils, how did you take that?" She said. "I mean I wouldn't have allowed him to touch me as drunk as he was."

"Well as drunk as he was, I thought it better to humor him, let him do a basic massage and pay him so he would leave. And you helped me get rid of him by playing opossum and pretending to be asleep."

"Yes, that's the least I could do, I don't want a massage. Who knows where his hands would end up? Oh, by the way did you hear about the big fight down at the market today?"

"No tell me! What happened?"

"Some Fijian villager had sold his yaqona (kava) to one of the Indian vendors at the market yesterday. He got his money and went out shopping. Today he came back into the market, went right up to the vendor, grabbed him by the throat and demanded his yaqona be returned. The Indian vendor told him he had already been paid and had his money. Then the villager punched the vendor in the face. One of the other Indian vendors, who was only half the Fijian's size jumped in to help his friend. Some Fijians grabbed the Indians and held them back but nobody held the Fijian man who kept boxing the vendors. The Indians finally broke loose and counterattacked. It was a real melee. Everyone watched. No one called the police. Finally, the Fijian's primary school-aged daughter pulled on his sleeve and urged him to leave because he would get hurt. From what everyone saw he wasn't the one getting hurt. Imagine that?"

"I think likely the man doesn't understand the difference between the wholesale price and the retail price. The Indians can't sell the Yaqona for more than the retail price but they can't make any money if they buy at retail so they pay somewhat less but buy large quantities. The man probably thinks the vendors should pay full retail. You know how too many people here think everybody else cheats even though they may be the ones cheating others. Cheating others is OK. Being cheated is not OK."

Well after midnight, the Little Woman turned the fan on partly to blow away mosquitos but mostly to make our bedroom cool enough to sleep. Having had too many rum sundowners, we collapsed into the bed in a half stupor. Although covered with only a sheet, we sweated in the still air and stifling heat. I wiped my brow to stop the trickle of sweat from flowing into my eyes.

I reminisced and waited for sleep. My memories were foggy, indistinct, and out of sequence. My thoughts turned to narrow, crushed coral roads crowded with pigs, little pigs strutting on the walkways, big pigs rooting in the gardens, tiny pigs chasing dogs and gigantic sows suckling piglets in the graveyard. My thoughts turned to the preschooler in the graveyard and his tear-filled eyes while the child's bigger kindergarten sister showered blows on the little tyke. The same feisty sister refused to hit her 10-year-old brother earlier that morning even though he slapped her across the face. And then I remembered something from earlier.

"We teach our children to respect their elders and never, never, never to hit them. It is OK for us to respectfully dispute something with an elder but never OK to physically abuse an elder." After recalling the interactions between the children, it was clear that what was explained to me applied even to children. Evidently, the prohibition against violence only went one way, up and not down.

Finally, I had a faint consciousness of heavy breathing and a small sweaty body next to me as I felt a heavy downward pull into sleep.

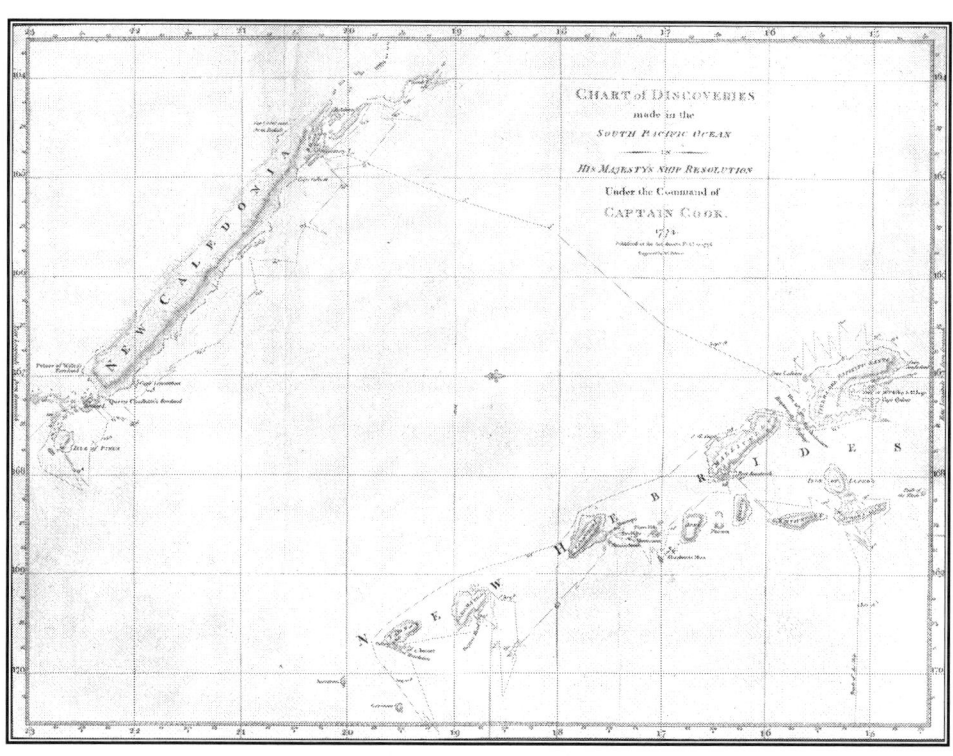

PART VII: NEW CALEDONIA

Chart of discoveries made in the South Pacific Ocean in his majesty's ship Resolution under the command of Captain Cook, 1774.
Published as the act directs Feby. 1st, 1776. Engraved by W. Palmer. Published Febry. 1st, 1777 by Wm. Strahan in New Street, Shoe Lane & Thos. Cadell in the Strand, London.

Man of New Caledonia.
Drawn from nature by W. Hodges. Engrav' by (Francois Germain?) Aliamet. No. XXXIX.
Published Feby. 1st, 1772 by Wm. Strahan in New Street Shoe Lane & Thos Cadell
in the Strand, London

View in the island of New Caledonia.
Drawn from nature by W. Hodges. Engraved by W. Byrne. No. L. Published Feb. 1st, 1777 by W. Strahan, New Street, Shoe Lane & Thos. Cadell in the Strand, London.

CHAPTER SIXTEEN

FIRE BOMBS, TEAR GAS AND ASSASSINATION

NEW CALEDONIA

A man in the van put a blindfold over my eyes. It was hardly necessary since I couldn't see where we were going in any case as the van had no windows. We drove around another 30 minutes until the van stopped. The man escorted me out of the van into another alley. He took off my blindfold. From there we went through a house then exited into another house.

S ITTING UNDER THE COCONUT TREE by the water's edge where the hot springs run into the bay turning the beach into a steam bath, my thoughts wandered back to my first weeks in-country and my first assignment decades before….and what had happened in the decades since that initial visit.

ଽଓ

"Nils," the Deputy Chief of Mission (DCM) said so many years ago. "I am assigning you to go to New Caledonia to do fact finding and report on the independence movement. It'll be a piece of cake assignment, a kind of first reporting experience for a rookie. No one will much notice what you report anyway since New Caledonia is so far off the beaten-track it virtually doesn't exist in terms of geopolitical or strategic importance."

As far as he was concerned, the DCM was sending me on a kind of an excursion more than anything else. Of course, he was wrong. It didn't turn out the way he described. Far from it.

In those days when I spent half of my life traveling from island to island across the Pacific I fixated on the airplanes that took me from place to place. Be they DC-3s with balloon tires for grass landing strips, four-seat puddle jumpers I flew in across Fiji or DC-10s across oceans, I was always interested in the plane, its comfort level and safety record. The flight to Nouméa, New Caledonia, later that week was aboard the French airline, Air Calédonie. The airline had begun regularly scheduled international service to Fiji in the mid 80's. The international airline was essentially a one airplane service that flew a 1950's era SE10-Caravelle with its iconic tear drop windows. While I had grown used to the ancient aircraft and even more ancient ferries and fishing boats that came to die in the Pacific islands, I was unprepared for the dismal looking, rear engine Caravelle. As I climbed the open-air stairs and boarded I could only describe the interior of the plane as shabby, somewhat torn up and very, very tired looking. I hoped it was still safe but since only one airline made the flight to the French colony, New Caledonia, I really had no choice. New or ancient. Clean or soiled. Safe or not. This was my flight. Little was I to know that the flight was to be the safest part of my travels.

On the ground as I trying to get a feel for New Caledonia's relationship with France, I quickly learned the indigenous Kanak independence movement was as fractured and as fragile as the different tribal factions that made up the resistance. I knew from my research that for decade factions such as the Front Indépendantiste, had seized farms from the early European settlers, the Caldoche, while the Front de Libération Kanak Socialiste (FLNKS) tried to set up a provisional government following prolonged violence. Meanwhile, to try to rid itself of the trouble, the Socialist government, in power at that time in France, tried, without avail, to placate the Kanaks, who already represented less than half of the population. Whatever the government in metropolitan France tried to do, it alienated one ethnic group or another in New Caledonia.

The second day I was in-country, violence erupted and escalated again. Even as I went from meeting to meeting to learn the intent of various leaders, the French National Gendarmerie Intervention Group, a special service arm of the French military attached to the police, tried to quell rioters with tear gas and water cannon. At one point, I parked my rental car when a group of rioters, chased by the Gendarmerie, ran around my car. As the wind turned I felt the sting of tear gas in my eyes as it seeped through edges of the car windows.

After the air cleared of tear gas I went on to my next interview with one of the Independence Movement only to find he was the nephew of another faction leader I had met the previous day. What he said was unremarkable but I did notice he had only a beautifully posed photo of just himself on his desk. There were no other photos in his office only a portrait of himself.

The third and final day in country, I had arranged to meet the most controversial and most secretive of the independence leaders. His contacts had arranged to pick me up at my hotel. As I waited till the appointed time, an attractive young part-European woman entered the lobby, walked toward me and called me by name.

"Yes," I answered.

"I am here to take you to your meeting. Please follow me."

Instead of going out the front door of the hotel she came in as I expected, she walked through the hotel lobby toward the back door to the parking lot. As we exited a car appeared at the exit door and we got in. We drove around for about an hour then turned into an alley and stopped behind a van blocking the way. We got out of the car and she motioned for me to get into the van in front of us. That was the last I saw of her.

A man in the van put a blindfold over my eyes. It was hardly necessary since I couldn't see where we were going in any case as the van had no windows. We drove around another 30 minutes until the van stopped. The man escorted me out of the van into another alley. He took off my blindfold. From there we went through a house then exited into another house. It was there I met the FLNKS faction leader, Jean-Marie Tjibaou. He spoke French and a little English while I spoke English and a little French. Somehow, we managed to communicate. At the end of the meeting I asked him about the rumors that he was a communist.

"Qui veut noyer son chien l'accuse d'avoir la rage." He said.

"Yes," I replied. "We have a similar expression in English. 'Give a dog a bad name and hang him.' I understand what you mean. Thank you for your time today."

Immediately, he left by the back door. I was escorted sans blindfold back to my hotel.

Shortly thereafter, the French government signed the Matignon Accord on 26 June 1988 with the same Jean-Marie Tjibaou and an anti-independence leader, Jacques Lafleur. The accord thus ensured French rule and a promise of an eventual referendum on independence. "A year later, in response to widespread feeling among Kanaks that they had been betrayed, Jean-Marie Tjibaou and his deputy were assassinated by a follower."

Any referendum on independence will be strongly supported by the indigenous but now 40 percent minority Kanak and resisted by the Caldoche and other ethnic groups. The Caldoche, mostly French descended from early settlers, are, other than the indigenous Kanaks, the group most vested in New Caledonia. It should be noted that unlike most Pacific Island States, with the exception of Fiji, New Caledonia has significant numbers of non-indigenous people. More recent immigrants are called Caledonians rather than Caldoche. Other nationalities include British, Irish, Italians, Germans, Belgians, Swiss, Spaniards, Croatians and Poles. Others are either mixed race or come from Indonesia, Vietnam, Japan, India and Algeria. Those from Algeria are either Berbers sent in the 19th century as prisoners or descendants from European settlers in former French colonies, the pieds noirs. As a group, the pieds noirs are vehemently anti-independence. All these groups including the Caldoche number nearly 60 per cent of the population.

My findings and conclusions that the independence movement was not likely to advance any time soon and that the French would remain for a long time to come were not popular at Embassy Paris. But the facts on the ground were clear even then. New Caledonia has 25% of the world's nickel reserves, a strategic metal, about a third of the GDP consisted of remittances from France. International mining companies had invested hundreds of millions of dollars and would invest hundreds of millions more. The economy depended upon France and nickel. France wanted to maintain its South Pacific military base. The Gendarmerie kept a lid on the resistance. It was obvious that France's interest was not to protect the Caldoche since the official French did not regard the Caldoche as French. France would stay because it was in France's interest. Indigenous Kanak independence leaders likely would be bought off or compromised.

༄༅

Postscript 2015: "The political climate has thus become crippled by decades of division. The violence of the 1980s and the uncompromising rhetoric of many independence activists have driven away moderates. In a population where some 40 percent of the 260,000 inhabitants are indigenous and 29 percent European, the FLNKS can scarcely afford to continue alienating the remaining 31 percent as the referendum approaches...."

We shall see.

ACKNOWLEDGMENTS

MANY THANKS to David for many edits and recommendations over too long a time, to Tess for cover design, helping me sort through multiple drafts and setting up an author's Facebook page and promotion. I am indebted to many anonymous Pacific Islanders and tellers of tales and to my email readers who put up with my many early drafts and made helpful suggestions.

Living in a small country has its advantages. Once I received a letter with only a two-line address. The first line was my name: the second Fiji Islands. In a miracle of miracles, it got to me. It was one of those moments when one feels inextricably important but truthfully, I think its arrival more a testament to the efficiency of Fiji Post than my renown. I write this having just said Bon Voyage to a 75-year-old Frenchman who has traveled to 128 countries and intends to travel to 60 more. I always thought I was a world traveler. My travel efforts pale beside this giant of the visa line. My wife enjoys papaya with some freshly squeezed lemon juice and yogurt. She calls it longevity fruit and is determined I should eat more of it. She has exhibited endless patience during the too long effort to complete this manuscript. Finishing it has given me the greatest sense pleasure since my mother discovered me as a five-year-old hiding under the kitchen table finishing off the last of six ice cream bars intended for the family after dinner dessert. I hope you'll get as much pleasure from these stories as I did from writing them.

Although this is a work of fiction the stories are liberally basted with facts from news articles, innuendo, first-hand accounts, observation and gossip. Names, dates and some locations have been changed to protect the innocent and sometimes the guilty. Artistic license abounds. Any resemblance to any person living or dead except for well-known persons in the public domain is merely coincidence.

ABOUT THE AUTHOR

GERALD ANDERSEN IS AN 'OLD ASIA HAND' having first moved to Asia in the late 1970's. He divides his travel time between Asia and the Pacific Islands. He has lived in 10 countries, worked in 20 and has traveled in more than 80 and counting.

As a diplomat lying abroad for his country he managed to punctuate his career with a series of exclamation marks. He was mugged and narrowly escaped a grenade attack in Phnom Penh, Cambodia, was in Fiji for the first of several coups, in Pakistan when President, Zia ul Haq, and the American Ambassador, Arnold Raphel, were killed in a suspicious plane crash, in the Republic of Georgia for the Rose Revolution, in Jordan at the death of King Hussein and the crowning of his son Abdullah II. His Sri Lanka apartment was surrounded by anti-aircraft fire when the Tamil Tiger Liberation Front bombed the capital, Colombo. Then there was the night sleeping in a bathtub during a rocket attack, and car bombs on the way to the airport in Kabul, Afghanistan. But those are other stories.

OTHER BOOKS BY THE AUTHOR
Happily Married to a Chinese National

Made in the USA
Columbia, SC
04 April 2019